The Truth About Stacey

ANN M. MARTIN

SCHOLASTIC INC.

*The author would like to
thank Dr. Claudia Werner
for her sensitive evaluation
of this manuscript.*

Copyright © 1986 by Ann M. Martin

This book was originally published in paperback by Scholastic Inc. in 1986.

All rights reserved. Published by Scholastic Inc., *Publishers since 1920.* SCHOLASTIC, THE BABY-SITTERS CLUB, and associated logos are trademarks and/or registered trademarks of Scholastic Inc.

The publisher does not have any control over and does not assume any responsibility for author or third-party websites or their content.

No part of this publication may be reproduced, stored in a retrieval system, or transmitted in any form or by any means, electronic, mechanical, photocopying, recording, or otherwise, without written permission of the publisher. For information regarding permission, write to Scholastic Inc., Attention: Permissions Department, 557 Broadway, New York, NY 10012.

ISBN 978-1-338-64222-3

10 9 8 7 6 5 4 3 2 1   20 21 22 23 24

Printed in the U.S.A. 40
This edition first printing 2020

Book design by Maeve Norton

CHAPTER 1

"As president of the Baby-sitters Club," said Kristy Thomas, "I hereby move that we figure out what to do when Mrs. Newton goes to the hospital to have her baby."

"What do you mean?" I said.

"Well, we ought to be prepared. We've been waiting for this baby for months, and the Newtons are practically our best clients. They'll need someone to take care of Jamie while his parents are at the hospital. Smart baby-sitters would be ready for the occasion."

"I think that's a good idea," spoke up Mary Anne Spier. "I second the motion." Mary Anne usually agrees with Kristy. After all, they're best friends.

I glanced across the room at Claudia Kishi. Claudia is *my* best friend, and vice president of our club. She shrugged her shoulders at me.

There are just the four of us in the Baby-sitters

Club: Kristy, Claudia, Mary Anne (she's the secretary), and me, Stacey McGill. I'm the treasurer. We've been in business for about two months. Kristy thought up the club, which was why she got to be president. We meet three times a week from five-thirty to six o'clock in Claudia's room (Claudia has a private phone), and our clients call then to line us up as sitters. The reason the club works so well is that with four baby-sitters there at the phone, each person who calls is pretty much guaranteed to get a sitter for whatever time he or she needs. Our clients like that. They say that having to make a whole bunch of calls just to line up one sitter is a waste of time. They like us, too. We're good baby-sitters. And we worked hard to get our business going. We printed up flyers and distributed them in mailboxes, and even put an ad in *The Stoneybrook News*, the voice of Stoneybrook, Connecticut.

That's where I live now, in this teeny-weeny town in Connecticut. Let me tell you, it's quite a shock after life in New York City. New York is a big place. Stoneybrook is not. There is only one middle school here, and I go to it. We all do. (We're in seventh grade.) In New York there are about a billion middle schools. In fact, in New York there are about a billion of everything—people, cars, buildings, stores, pigeons, friends, and things to do.

Here there's, well, there's . . . not much, really. My parents and I moved into our house in August and I didn't make a single friend until I met Claudia in school in September. Everyone here seems to have known everyone else since they were babies. Claudia, Kristy, and Mary Anne have. And they've grown up together, since Kristy and Mary Anne live next door to each other on Bradford Court and Claudia lives across the street from them. (I live two streets away.)

So, was I ever glad when Claudia told me Kristy wanted to start the club! Friends at last, I thought. And that's just what I found. Even though I'm better friends with Claudia, I don't know what I'd do without Kristy and Mary Anne. It's true that they seem younger than Claudia and me (they don't care much about clothes or boys yet—although Kristy *did* just go to her first dance), and Mary Anne is unbelievably shy, and Kristy's sort of a tomboy. But they're my friends, and I belong with them. Which is more than I can say about certain traitors I left behind in New York.

"All right, here's one plan," Kristy was saying. "It's a school afternoon. Mrs. Newton realizes that it's time to go to the hospital. She calls Mr.

Newton or a cab or whatever, then calls us, and one of us goes to stay with Jamie."

"What if we're all busy?" I asked.

"Hmm," said Kristy. "Maybe from now on, one of us should be free each afternoon so Mrs. Newton will be guaranteed a baby-sitter. It will be a special service for her, since the Newtons are such good customers."

"That seems like kind of a waste," spoke up Claudia, which was exactly what I was thinking.

"That's right," I said. "Babies can be late. Two or three weeks late. We could be giving up an awful lot of perfectly good afternoons for nothing."

"That's true," said Kristy thoughtfully.

"How about a nighttime plan?" I suggested. "Doesn't it seem that pregnant women always rush off to the hospital in the middle of the night? I was born at two-twenty-two A.M."

"I was born at four-thirty-six A.M.," said Claudia.

"I was born at four A.M. on the dot," said Kristy.

We looked at Mary Anne. She shrugged. "I don't know what time I was born." Mary Anne's mother died when Mary Anne was little, and Mary Anne is not very close to her strict father. It figures that they'd never talked about the day (or night) she was born.

A knock came on Claudia's door. Mimi, her grandmother, stuck her head in the room. "Hello, girls," she said politely.

"Hi, Mimi," we answered.

"May I offer you something to eat?" she asked. Claudia's family is Japanese, and Mimi, who didn't come to the United States until she was thirty-two years old, speaks with a gentle, rolling accent. She has lived with Claudia's family since before Claudia was born.

"No thanks, Mimi," replied Claudia, "but maybe you could help us."

"Certainly." Mimi opened the door the rest of the way and stood just inside the room.

"Do you know what time Mary Anne was born?" Claudia asked. She figured Mimi would know since Claudia's parents have been friendly with the Thomases and the Spiers for years, and Mimi had gotten to know the families, too.

Mimi looked only slightly taken aback. "Let me think for a moment, my Claudia. . . . Mary Anne, your mother and father left for the hospital around dinnertime. That I remember clearly. I believe you were born near eleven o'clock."

"Oh!" A grin lit up Mary Anne's face. "I didn't know. So I was another nighttime baby. Thank you, Mimi."

"It was my pleasure." Mimi turned to leave, and almost bumped into Janine, Claudia's sister, who had come up behind her.

"Claudia! Claudia!" cried Janine.

I looked up in alarm. Janine is this prim, not-much-fun fifteen-year-old who's a genius. To be honest, she's boring. Dull as dishwater. I'd never even heard her raise her voice, which was why, the minute I heard her cry "Claudia!" I knew something was wrong. Very wrong.

Unfortunately, I was right.

"Janine! What is it?" exclaimed Claudia.

"This." Janine was waving a paper around. She squeezed past Mimi and thrust it at Claudia.

Claudia took it, and Kristy, Mary Anne, and I crowded around. We stared at the paper in horror. This is what we saw:

Need a reliable baby-sitter?
Need one fast?
Then call:
THE BABY-SITTERS AGENCY
Liz Lewis: 555-1162
OR
Michelle Patterson: 555-7548
And reach a whole network of responsible
baby-sitters!

Ages: 13 and up
Available:
After school
Weekends (until midnight)
Weeknights (until 11:00)
Low rates! Years of experience!
The ultimate time-saver!
CALL NOW!

The four of us just looked at each other. Even Kristy, who has sort of a big mouth, couldn't say anything. Mary Anne's eyes grew so wide I thought they would pop right out of her head.

"What is wrong, my Claudia?" asked Mimi.

"Competition," Claudia replied stiffly.

Kristy checked her watch and saw that it was only five-forty-five, and that we still had fifteen minutes left to our Friday meeting. "I hereby change this meeting of the Baby-sitters Club to an emergency meeting," she announced.

"We will leave you alone, then," said Mimi softly. "Janine, please help me with dinner." Mimi tiptoed out, followed by Janine, who closed the door softly behind her.

I looked at my three stricken friends.

Claudia's dark eyes were troubled. She was absentmindedly playing with a strand of her long black hair. Claudia is very fashion conscious and always dresses in the absolute latest trendy clothes, but I could tell that clothes were the last things on her mind.

Kristy, wearing her typical little-girl clothes, her brown hair pulled back into a messy pony-tail, looked as troubled as Claudia did.

Mary Anne, her hair in braids as usual (her father makes her wear it that way), had put on her wire-rimmed glasses to read the flyer. When she was finished, she sighed, leaned back against the wall, and kicked off her penny loafers.

If I could have looked at myself, I would have seen a second trendy dresser and a fourth long face, more sophisticated than Kristy's or Mary Anne's but not nearly as beautiful as Claudia's.

I examined a pink-painted nail while Kristy held the dreadful flyer in her shaking hand.

"We're dead," she said to no one in particular. "The other baby-sitters are older than we are. They can stay out later than we can. We're doomed."

Not one of us disagreed with her.

In nervous desperation, Claudia took a shoe box from under her bed, reached in, and pulled out a roll of Life Savers. Claudia is a junk-food addict (although she won't admit it), and she has candy and snacks stashed all around her bedroom, along with the Nancy Drew books her parents disapprove of because they think they're not "quality" reading. She was so upset about the Baby-sitters Agency that when she was passing around the Life Savers, she forgot and offered *me* a piece. I'm diabetic and absolutely not allowed to eat extra sweets. I used to try to keep my illness a secret from people, but Claudia, Mary Anne, and Kristy know about it, and they don't usually offer me candy.

"Who *are* Liz Lewis and Michelle Patterson?" asked Mary Anne, peering over to look at the flyer again.

I shrugged. I barely knew the kids in my homeroom, let alone in any other grade.

"Maybe they don't go to the middle school," suggested Kristy. "It says the baby-sitters are thirteen and up. Liz and Michelle probably go to the high school. I wonder if Sam or Charlie knows them." (Charlie and Sam are Kristy's older brothers. They're sixteen and fourteen. She has a little brother, too, David Michael, who's six.)

"No, they go to Stoneybrook Middle School," spoke up Claudia, in a tone of voice that indicated she was likely to expire in a few seconds. "They're eighth-graders."

"They must be pretty friendly with the high school kids," I said, "unless there are a whole bunch of really old eighth-graders that we don't know about."

Claudia snorted. "For all I know, there are. Liz and Michelle could be fourteen or fifteen. I wish you guys knew who they are. You'd faint. Those two aren't baby-sitters any more than I'm the queen of France."

"What's wrong with them?" I asked.

"For one thing, I wouldn't trust them farther than I could throw a truck," said Claudia. "They have smart mouths, they sass the teachers, they hate school, they hang around at the mall. You know, *that* kind of kid."

"It doesn't mean they're not good baby-sitters," said Mary Anne.

"I'd be surprised if they were," replied Claudia.

"I wonder how the agency works," mused Kristy. She was still holding the flyer. "There are only two names on this, but it says you can get in touch with 'a whole network of responsible baby-sitters.' I'll say one thing, Liz and Michelle know how to go after customers. Their flyer is a lot better than ours was."

"Hmph," I said.

"Hey!" cried Mary Anne. "I have an idea. Let's call the agency and pretend we need a sitter. Maybe we can find out how those girls operate." Mary Anne may be shy, but she sure can come up with daring ideas.

"Oh, that's smart!" said Kristy approvingly. "I'll make up a name and say I need a baby-sitter for my younger brother. Then I can call them back later and cancel."

"Okay," Claudia and I agreed.

"Competition, are you ready?" Kristy asked the phone. "Here comes the Baby-sitters Club!"

CHAPTER 2

Kristy called Liz Lewis, just because Liz was listed first on the flyer. She put her hand over the mouthpiece. "It's ringing," she whispered to us. "One . . . two . . . thr— Hello? Is Liz Lewis there, please? . . . Oh, hi, Liz. My name is—Candy. Candy Kane. . . . No, no joke. . . . I got your flyer for the Baby-sitters Agency. I'm supposed to sit for my little brother tomorrow and" (Kristy paused, and the rest of us watched the wheels turning) "I just got asked out on a date."

Mary Anne started to giggle. She grabbed a pillow from Claudia's bed and buried her face in it to muffle the sounds. Kristy turned away so she wouldn't have to see.

"From three to five," Kristy was saying. (Liz must have asked her when she was supposed to be sitting.) "He's seven years old. His name is, um, Harry. . . . Twenty-eight Roper Road. Will *you* be baby-sitting for him? The flyer said—Oh,

I see. . . . Mm-hmm. . . . I'll be at 555-3231. Oh, but only for about ten minutes. Then I have—I have another date. . . . Who with?"

By that time, Claudia was laughing, too, and I was on the verge of it. Kristy glanced at us helplessly, not sure what to do about her "date." Then she simply pulled a name out of the air. "With Winston Churchill," she replied, taking the chance that Liz wouldn't know who he was. Apparently she didn't. "Yeah, he goes to high school," continued Kristy nonchalantly, getting into her story. "A sophomore. Football player . . . Me? I'm in seventh. . . . Yeah, I know."

I had to leave the room. I couldn't stand it any longer, and I didn't want to ruin Kristy's call. I closed Claudia's door, ran to the bathroom, laughed, and returned.

Kristy was saying, "Okay, five minutes . . . Yeah, later." She hung up. Then she began to laugh, too. "You guys!" she exclaimed. "Don't do that to me when I'm on the phone."

"But *Winston Churchill*?" I cried. "The high school guy you're *dating*?"

When we calmed down, Kristy said, "All right, this is how I think the agency works. People call Liz and Michelle when they need sitters. Then Liz and Michelle simply turn around and *find* the sitters. In other words, they do all the phoning for their clients. I guess they must baby-sit, too, from time to time. But when they don't, they probably get part of the salary earned by the sitter they found for the job."

"No wonder their sitters are so old," said Mary Anne. "All Liz and Michelle have to do is *call* older kids."

"Yeah," said Kristy glumly. "We could do that ourselves, if we'd thought of it." She paused. "Liz seemed more interested in my date than in finding a baby-sitter."

"Figures," said Claudia.

The phone rang. "I'll get it. It's probably Liz," said Kristy. Mary Anne got ready with a pillow. "Hello, the B—hello?" (Kristy had almost said, "Hello, the Baby-sitters Club," which is how we answer the phone during meetings.) "Yes, this is she. . . . Oh, terrific. . . . *How* many? . . . Wow. How old are they? . . . Okay. . . . Patricia Clayton. . . . Okay. . . . Okay, thanks a lot. I'll see Patricia tomorrow. . . . Later." She hung up.

"Later?" repeated Mary Anne.

"That's how Liz says good-bye."

"So?" I asked.

"She actually found three available sitters," said Kristy. "She gave me a choice. I didn't know any of the names, but two were thirteen years old, and one was fifteen years old. One was even a *boy*. I chose the fifteen-year-old. People are going to *love* the agency. I'm not kidding. We don't offer a range of ages like they do. There are no boys in our club. And we can't stay out past ten, even on the weekends."

We looked at each other sadly.

At last, Mary Anne stood up. "It's after six. I've got to go home." Mr. Spier likes Mary Anne home on the dot. I was surprised she was letting herself be even a few minutes late. It just showed how upset she was.

"I might as well go, too," I said.

"Yeah," said Kristy.

The three of us said good-bye to Claudia and left. "See you guys!" called Mary Anne when we reached the Kishis' stoop. She was suddenly in a hurry. Across the street I could see her father standing at their front door.

"Well," I said to Kristy.

"Well."

"Kristy, we'll make it. We're good baby-sitters."

"I know," she said. But that was *all* she said. I kind of expected Kristy to be a little more positive. I mean, the club was really more hers than anybody else's. I thought she'd do anything for the club. I would.

But maybe that was because the club was more than just a project or a business to me. It was my friends. It was the only good thing that had happened to me in the last horrible year.

I ran home.

Somehow, I managed to eat dinner that night. It wasn't easy. For one thing, ever since I developed the diabetes and I've had to watch what I eat so carefully, food simply isn't much fun anymore. Often when I'm hungry, I don't care *what* I eat. I eat just to fill up. And since I was upset about the Baby-sitters Agency that night, I wasn't even hungry. But Mom watches my food intake like a hawk, particularly since I've lost a little weight recently. So I forced down what I thought was a reasonable dinner.

As soon as I could, I escaped to my room. I closed my door and sat down in my armchair to think. It had been just a year earlier that I had started to show the symptoms of diabetes. At first, we didn't think anything was wrong. I was hungry all the time—I mean, *really* hungry, nothing could fill me up—and thirsty, too. "Well, you're a growing girl," Mom had said. "I expect this is the beginning of a growth spurt. Let's measure you." Sure enough, I'd grown an inch and a half.

But then, even though I was eating and eating, I began to lose weight. I didn't feel well, either. I grew tired easily and sometimes I felt weak all over. Twice, I wet my bed. (The second time, I happened to be sharing a double bed with my former best friend, Laine Cummings, at a sleepover.) When that happened, Mom forgot about my growth spurt and decided I was having a psychological problem. She took me to a fancy New York psychiatrist. During my first session with him, he asked me about the bed-wetting, heard that I was losing weight, and watched me drink three sodas. He was the one who realized what was going on and told Mom to make an appointment with my pediatrician. Mom did. Two weeks later, I was learning how to give myself insulin and monitor my blood sugar level.

Diabetes is a problem with a gland in your body called the pancreas. The pancreas makes insulin, which is a hormone. What insulin does is use the sugar and starch that your body takes in when you eat to give you heat and energy and to break down other foods. When the pancreas doesn't make enough insulin to do the job, then glucose from the sugars and starches builds up in your blood and makes you sick. And not just a little sick. If you don't treat diabetes properly, you could *die*.

Well, *I* practically died when I first heard that. But then the doctor explained that you can give yourself insulin every day to keep the right amount in your body. When you take insulin and control your diet, you can lead a normal life.

It was a lot of responsibility. I would have to watch what I ate *and* make sure I was getting the right amount of insulin. As much as they wanted to, Mom or Dad couldn't always do that for me. Still, I feel weird having to check (or sometimes inject) insulin in front of my friends. I don't like the thought of them thinking I'm sick.

Before I got diabetes, I really had it pretty easy. I'm an only child. For as long as I could remember, I'd lived in a large apartment in a nice, safe building with a doorman on the Upper West Side in New York City. I had my own bedroom with windows that looked out over Central Park. I went to a private school. I didn't have any pets, and, of course, no brothers or sisters, but I wasn't lonely. I had lots of friends at school and in my building, and my parents let me invite them over whenever I wanted. Mom and Dad seemed to be pretty cool parents—a little pushy, maybe, and more involved in my life than I liked, but that was it. They let me dress the way I wanted, go out with my friends after school, and play my stereo at top volume as long as the neighbors didn't complain.

Then, right before I began to get sick, Mom found out that she and Dad couldn't have any more children. They'd been trying for a long time, but they hadn't been able to have a brother or sister for me. It was unfortunate that they got that news just before I got the diabetes. What if I died? I'd be gone and they wouldn't be able to have another child. Suddenly, they were faced with the possibility of *no* children — no children of their own, anyway.

That was sad, but the upshot of it was that, practically overnight, Mom and Dad became the world's two most overprotective parents — and not just where food and insulin were concerned. Suddenly, they began to worry about me when I wasn't home. Mom would call me at my friends' apartments after school to make sure I was all right. She even called me at school every noon until the headmistress suggested that it wasn't very healthy for me, and reminded Mom about the nice, qualified school nurse.

Then began the business with the doctors. My parents became convinced that they could find either a miracle cure or a better treatment for me. They never doubted that I had diabetes; they just couldn't leave it alone. They made Helping Stacey their new goal in life.

Unfortunately, they weren't helping me at all. I was losing friends fast, and being yanked out of school to see some new doctor every time I turned around didn't make things any better. Laine Cummings began to hate me the night I wet the bed we were sharing. I didn't blame her for being mad, but why did she have to be mad for so long? We'd been best friends since we were five. Laine said that the real reason she was mad was that I had spent a lot of time at the slumber party that night talking to Allison Ritz, a new girl. But I don't know. Laine acted strange after I wet the bed, stranger still the first time I had to stay in the hospital, and even stranger after I started going to all those doctors. Maybe I should have told her about the diabetes, but for some reason, my parents kept the truth a secret from their friends, so I did the same. In fact, I didn't tell anyone the truth until we left New York and started over again in Connecticut. I finally told Claudia, Kristy, and Mary Anne my secret. But Laine still doesn't know, and even though her parents are my parents' best friends, they don't know, either. I don't see what the big deal is, but I guess it doesn't matter now.

At the beginning of my illness, hospital visits couldn't be avoided. I needed tests, I had to have my diet and insulin regulated, and once I fainted at school and went into insulin shock and the ambulance came and took me to St. Luke's. If one of my friends got that sick, I would have called her in the hospital and sent her cards and visited her when she went home. But not Laine. She seemed almost afraid of me (although she tried to cover up by acting cool and snooty). And my other friends did what Laine did, because she was the leader. Their leader. My leader. And we were her followers.

The school year grew worse and worse. I fainted twice more at school, each time causing a big scene and getting lots of attention, and every week, it seemed, I missed at least one morning while Mom and Dad took me to some doctor or clinic or other. Laine called me a baby, a liar, a hypochondriac, and a bunch of other things that indicated she thought my parents and I were making a big deal over nothing.

But if she *really* thought it was nothing, why wouldn't she come over to my apartment anymore? Why wouldn't she share sandwiches or go to the movies with me? And why did she move her desk away from mine in school? I was confused and unhappy and sick, and I didn't have any friends left, thanks to Laine.

I hated Laine.

In May, Mom and Dad announced that we were moving to Connecticut. I didn't have any friends there, but I didn't have any left in New York, either, so what did it matter? They said they were moving because Dad wanted to transfer to a different branch of the company he worked for, but somehow I knew they were moving partly because of me—to get me out of the city, away from the sooty air and the dirt and the noise, away from all the bad times and bad memories. They were overreacting and I knew it.

But I didn't care.

CHAPTER 3

I might have continued to moon away all evening, except that my thoughts (all by themselves) suddenly turned to something much more interesting: boys. All boys are pretty interesting, but I like two in particular. One is Kristy's brother Sam. He's the one who's fourteen, a freshman at Stoneybrook High. I know he liked *me* the first time we met. I was baby-sitting for Kristy's little brother, and Sam came home, and his jaw nearly fell off his face when he saw me in the kitchen. I thought he was cute, too, and my own jaw nearly fell off. We had fun together that day, but not much has happened since. I don't know why. I look exactly the same, I haven't done anything to offend him, and although I go over to Kristy's sometimes, hoping to see Sam, I never bug him. Maybe I'm just too young for him.

I don't worry about him much, though. I have a sort-of boyfriend in my own grade now. His name is Pete Black. He and I had been sitting at the same lunch table with Claudia and the other kids in the group she introduced me to—Dori, Emily, Rick, and Howie—since almost the beginning of school, but nothing special had happened with Pete until a couple of weeks ago, when he asked me to go to the Halloween Hop with him. Of course I said yes, and we went and had a wonderful time. Now we always sit next to each other in the cafeteria, and some evenings, Pete phones me just to talk.

"Knock, knock," called a voice from the other side of my bedroom door.

Mom.

I didn't really feel like talking to her.

"Can I come in?" she asked.

"Okay."

"Honey, are you feeling all right?" She asked the question even before she sat down on my bed.

"Yes. Fine." I hear that question about ten times a day.

"You didn't eat much dinner tonight."

"I wasn't hungry."

Mom began to look panicked. "You weren't snacking over at Claudia's, were you?"

"*Mother.* Of course not." The thing is, I *am*

allowed a certain amount of sweet stuff each day. In fact, I *have* to eat a certain amount of sweets in order to maintain that delicate balance between food and insulin. My diet is so exact, though, that I can't just snack whenever I feel like it. I can't, for instance, suddenly decide to eat a Twinkie or something over at Claudia's and then make up for it by giving myself extra insulin. It just doesn't work. In fact, it's a good way to make myself sick. So you can see why Mom panicked at the thought of my snacking. But for heaven's sake, doesn't she trust me? *I* don't want to get sick, either.

"Honey, I was just asking. . . . Are you really feeling fine?"

"*Yes.*"

"But you've lost three pounds."

"I can't help it. Maybe I'm more active now that I have some friends. Maybe we need to increase my diet."

"Are you hungry all the time?"

"Not all the time. Not like I was before we knew I had diabetes. But sometimes it seems like an awfully long time from one meal to the next."

"You weren't hungry tonight, though."

"No. . . ." I didn't want to talk about the Baby-sitters Club.

"Well, I'll call the doctor on Monday."

"Which one?" My main doctor, the specialist my pediatrician sent me to when the diabetes was first discovered, is in New York. Her name is Dr. Werner. But of course I have to have a doctor here in Stoneybrook, too, so Dr. Werner referred us to Dr. Frank. Both doctors are nice, but I like Dr. Werner better.

"I'll call Dr. Frank, I guess," said Mom. "I don't think we need to bother Dr. Werner."

I nodded.

Mom opened her mouth to say something, then closed it, hesitating. After a few more silent seconds, she said, "Just so you're prepared, dear—"

I cringed. Whatever was coming didn't sound good.

"— I want you to know that you're going to be scheduled for a series of tests with a new doctor in New York at the beginning of December."

I groaned.

"He's someone Uncle Eric heard about on a television program."

"We're going to a doctor because Uncle Eric saw him on TV?" I exclaimed.

"Honey, supposedly he's working miracles with diabetes. After Uncle Eric saw him, I found two articles about him in medical journals, and then *Profiles* magazine did a long interview with him. It was very impressive. He's getting a lot of attention right now."

"Did Dr. Werner say we should go see him?"

"No."

"Dr. Frank?"

"No."

"Have you even discussed this with them?"

"No."

"But, Mom, *why*? Why do I have to see another new doctor? There's no way to treat what I've got except with the diet and the insulin, and that's just what we're doing."

"There are always new developments, Stacey," said Mom quietly. "Your father and I want the best for you."

"We've *got* the best."

"It's only for three days."

"Three days! Three *days*? Do you know how much school I'll miss? And it'll all be for nothing. It always is. I spent sixth grade falling farther and farther behind, trying to keep up. Now I've started over in a new place, away from New York City, and you're going to keep dragging me back there and ruining my life? Mom, it's not fair."

"Hey, hey, hey. What's going on here?" Dad poked his head in my door.

"The doctors, Dad. More doctors. I don't mind

going to New York to see Dr. Werner, but don't make me keep looking for a miracle. Miracles don't happen. If *you* want to look, fine, but don't make me search with you."

"Young lady," said my father. "I don't appreciate your tone of voice."

I didn't answer him.

"We're doing this because we love you," said Mom.

"I know."

"We want what's best for you," added Dad.

"I *know*."

"All right." Dad sounded tired.

"I'll tell you about the new doctor some other time," said Mom. My parents left the room.

As soon as they closed the door, I heard the phone ring. A few seconds later, Dad called, "Stacey! For you."

"Coming!" I shouted.

I picked up the extension in my parents' bedroom, since Mom and Dad were downstairs. "Hello?" Half of me hoped the caller was Pete. The other half hoped for Sam Thomas.

It was Kristy. "Hi," she said glumly. "I've been thinking."

"Oh, good! About the club, I hope."

"What else? We didn't get nearly enough done

28

at our meeting this afternoon. I think we need to hold a special planning session."

"Great idea. I'll do anything for the club."

"Hey, thanks!" said Kristy. She sounded slightly less grim.

"Sure," I said. "I don't want anything to happen to the club." Oh, boy. If she only knew how *badly* I didn't want anything to happen to it.

"Tomorrow morning, eleven o'clock, club headquarters," said Kristy. (The club headquarters, of course, are in Claudia's bedroom.)

"I'll see you then," I said. We hung up.

I thought about our club problem for a long time before I fell asleep that night.

The next day, Kristy was running in high gear. I'd never seen her so hyper. For one thing, instead of sprawling on the floor the way she usually did during a meeting, she took over Claudia's desk, sitting up very tall in the straight-backed chair. For another thing, she was wearing a visor. And she was holding a clipboard and had stuck a pencil over her ear.

Mary Anne, who was perched in a director's chair, exchanged glances with Claudia and me on the bed. I could tell that Mary Anne and Claudia wanted to laugh at Kristy's overzealousness. But for some reason, I didn't.

"All right, the meeting will come to order," said Kristy brusquely. Mary Anne and Claudia calmed down. I gave my full attention to Kristy.

"Now," she began, one foot tapping insistently against a chair leg, "I've drawn up a list of ways to improve ourselves as baby-sitters and make us look better to our clients.

"Number one, we will do housework at no extra charge. Our clients will get the benefits of mother's helpers at baby-sitters' prices."

Claudia groaned. "I *hate* housework."

"Do you want to start losing jobs to Liz and Michelle?" Kristy asked her crisply.

"No," grumbled Claudia.

"Number two," continued Kristy, "we will offer special deals to our best customers."

I nodded my head vigorously.

"Number three, we will each make up a 'Kid-Kit' to bring with us when we sit."

"What's a 'Kid-Kit'?" asked Claudia.

"I was just about to explain," said Kristy.

"It's something that will not only make us look like dedicated baby-sitters to the parents but will be really fun for the kids. You know how you like to go over to your friends' houses because your friends always seem to have better stuff than you do? Better food, better things to do, and—when you were little—better toys?"

"Oh, yes!" I exclaimed. "In New York I had this friend named Laine. I loved to go to her apartment because her mother would buy Milky Way bars and keep them in the freezer. Biting into one of those was like biting into a frozen chocolate milk sha—"

I broke off, realizing that Claudia, Kristy, and Mary Anne were staring at me.

"Oh, well, that was be*fore* I got sick," I added. "Anyway, I know what you mean."

"Yeah," said Mary Anne. "I like Kristy's house because of her big family and Louie." (Louie is the Thomases' collie.)

"When I was a kid, I liked your house, Claud, because of all those board games you used to have," said Kristy, smiling. "Anyway, what we really like is the change of pace—new things or different things. So I thought, what better way to make a kid happy than to bring him some new things? Not *really* new, but new to the kid, and not to keep, of course, just to play with while we're there. The kids will *want us* to baby-sit because we'll be like a walking toy store. They probably won't even want us to leave, which should look good to the parents.

"See, what each of us will do is decorate a carton and label it 'Kid-Kit.' When we're going to sit somewhere, we'll fill it with games, toys, and books of our own, plus some things like paper and crayons that we'll have to replace from time to time. We can pay for them with our club dues. Then we'll each bring the kit along with us. The kids will love it."

"Great idea!" I said.

"I do have two more thoughts," Kristy went on.

She was speaking hesitantly, and I noticed Claudia glance at her sharply.

"Number four is lower rates." (This caused another groan from Claudia.) "*Just enough* lower," said Kristy defensively, "to undercut the Baby-sitters Agency."

"But we don't know what they earn," I protested.

"We will soon," said Kristy. "I'll find out. And number five is . . . is to do what the agency does—take on late jobs or jobs we can't handle by giving them to older kids. Sam and Charlie baby-sit sometimes, and Janine cou—"

"NO!" cried Claudia. "No. Kristy, this is getting out of hand. The Kid-Kit is a good idea, but lower rates and housework and giving away our jobs? No, no, no. If that's what this club is going to become, then I don't want to be in it."

"Me, neither," said Mary Anne softly.

Not be in the club? If both of them left, there wouldn't *be* any more club. They didn't mean it. They didn't *really* mean it. What would I do without the club? Talking to Pete on the phone was nice, and sitting with the group in the cafeteria was fun, but those kids weren't true friends like Claudia and Kristy and Mary Anne.

I needed the club.

"You guys," I said, "I don't want the Baby-sitters Club to fall apart. We can't let Liz and Michelle beat us. We have to prove that we can succeed, too."

"Yes," agreed Claudia, "but not the way Kristy said. That's—that's—what's the word?"

"Degrading?" suggested Mary Anne.

"Yes. That's it. Degrading."

"Well, what do *you* think we should do," snapped Kristy, "since you know so much?"

"I think," said Claudia, "that we should use two of your ideas—the Kid-Kit and the special deals—and save the other things, especially number five, as last resorts."

"That sounds like a good plan," said Mary

Anne. "Anyway, we wouldn't want to use up all your ideas at once."

"That's true," I said.

"All right," said Kristy with a sigh. She sent me a troubled look. I shrugged. Kristy knew I was on her side, but we both realized that we shouldn't overdo things.

"Come on," said Claudia. "Let's start making the Kid-Kit boxes now. It'll be fun! You guys each get a box from home and come back here. I have pastels and fabric and paints and all sorts of things we can decorate them with." (Claudia loves art.)

"We'll make the best boxes ever!" I said, trying to sound enthusiastic. "In fact, we'll be the best baby-sitters ever! Let's get to work!"

CHAPTER 4

The following Monday was a glorious, warm day that felt more like May than the middle of November. At exactly three-thirty, armed with my Kid-Kit, I rang the bell at Charlotte Johanssen's house. Charlotte, who's seven, is one of my favorite baby-sitting kids. Her mother is a doctor and her father is an engineer. Charlotte is an only child who's very smart but is shy and doesn't have many friends. I can sympathize when she gets lonely.

Dr. Johanssen answered the door. "Hello, Stacey," she said cheerfully, even though she looked quite tired. That Monday must have been one of her days off, because Dr. Johanssen is usually working at Stoneybrook General Hospital. Her schedule changes from month to month.

"Hi!" I replied.

"How have you been feeling?" Dr. Johanssen always asks me that. When anyone else asks,

I get annoyed, but not with Charlotte's mother.

"Hungry," I said honestly. "And I've lost some weight."

"Any problems with your insulin or your blood sugar level?"

"Nope. I think I just need to eat more. After all, I am twelve."

"That sounds sensible. What are you doing about the problem, though?"

"Mom called Dr. Frank today, but she hasn't been able to talk to him yet. I guess she'll know something by the time I get home."

"Stacey! Hi, Stacey!" Charlotte bounced into the hallway, beaming. She's always glad to see me.

"Hi, there," I said.

"What's that box?"

"Something special. I'll open it as soon as your mom leaves."

"Mom, go, go!" cried Charlotte. She never wants her parents to leave, even when I'm the baby-sitter.

"Is that a hint?" asked Dr. Johanssen, pulling on a sweater.

"I think so," I said.

"All right, girls. This meeting will be a quickie, I hope. I should be home between five and five-thirty."

"See you later, Mom." Charlotte practically pushed her mother out the door. "Now?" she asked me.

"Just let me take my jacket off." I hung it in the front hall closet while Charlotte hopped impatiently from one foot to the other. Then we sat down on the floor in the living room.

"Can you read what this says?" I asked, pointing to the words on the lid.

Charlotte leaned over for a better look. "'Kid-Kit,'" she said promptly. "It's pretty." I had covered my box with blue flowered fabric and glued white rickrack along the borders. Then I had cut the letters for "Kid-Kit" from green felt.

"Thanks. I'll bring this with me every time I baby-sit." I lifted the lid. "There's all sorts of fun stuff in here. And I'll change it once a month."

"Oh, neat," said Charlotte softly as she pulled the things out of the box. "Chutes and Ladders . . . Spill and Spell . . . *The Cricket in Times Square.* What's this book about?"

"Oh, you'll love it, I think. It's about a cricket named Chester who accidentally winds up in the middle of New York City and makes friends with a mouse named Tucker, a cat named Harry, and a boy named Mario. We can read a little each time I baby-sit. And I can tell you about New York."

Charlotte loves to hear about when I lived in the city. "And after we finish that book, we can read *Tucker's Countryside* and *Harry Cat's Pet Puppy*, which are more stories about those animals."

"Goody." Charlotte continued to look through the crayons and chalk and drawing paper, the jigsaw puzzle and Colorforms and jacks.

"We can do anything you want," I said, "but even though I brought the Kid-Kit, I have one other idea."

"What?"

"We could walk downtown. It's such a beautiful day. We could look in the store windows and find out what's playing at the movie theater, and maybe stop off at your school playground on the way home."

Charlotte looked as if someone were holding out two huge ice-cream cones, each made from one of her favorite flavors, and telling her she could have only one of them. She glanced out the window at the sunshine, pawed through the box once more, and then looked at me. "Downtown," she said at last, "if you promise to bring the Kid-Kit back."

I crossed my heart. "Promise."

So we put our jackets on and walked toward town. The center of Stoneybrook is about half a mile from Charlotte's house. We could run there in ten minutes or walk there (fast) in under twenty, but we dawdled along, taking our time. Charlotte kept stopping to pick up acorns.

"I should save these," she said. "Then if I ever got a pet squirrel, I could feed them to him."

"Now, what would you do with a pet squirrel?" I asked her.

"Talk to him."

"But you have Carrot. You can talk to him." (Carrot is the Johanssens' schnauzer.)

"It would be nice to have more than one person to talk to."

"Don't you have any friends, Charlotte? I mean, people-friends?"

Charlotte shook her head. She stooped down, picked up a particularly fat acorn, and stuffed it in her pocket as she stood up.

I looked at Charlotte. She's pretty—chestnut brown hair, big, dark eyes, and dimples in her cheeks when she smiles. She's smart, she's considerate, and she's sweet. So what was wrong with her? Why didn't she have any friends?

"The kids don't like me," she said, "and I don't like them."

"The kids in your class?" I asked. "Why don't you like them?"

"Because they don't like me."

"All right, why don't they like you?"

Charlotte shrugged. Then she stuck one thumb in her mouth and put her other hand in mine. We walked in silence until we reached the town.

"What shall we do?" I asked.

Charlotte perked up. She took her thumb out of her mouth. "The candy store!"

"Okay." Polly's Fine Candy is pretty spectacular as candy stores go. It's even better than a lot of candy stores in New York. I could understand why Charlotte wanted to go to it. It's a sort of fairyland. And in November, with the holidays just around the corner, it was more spectacular than usual.

The only thing I don't like about Polly's Fine Candy is Polly. She runs the store and is about a hundred years old. Her younger sister, who looks every bit as old as Polly, helps her. Any time kids go in the store, they fasten their eyeballs on them and don't take them off until the kids leave. But Charlotte and I were prepared to brave the sisters.

We approached the store. Long before we reached the doorway, we could smell chocolate. We breathed it in.

"Mmm, heavenly," I said.

"Yeah, heavenly," echoed Charlotte.

We looked in the windows. One was ready for Thanksgiving. The biggest chocolate turkey I'd ever seen was surrounded by smaller chocolate turkeys. They were standing in a bed of candy corn and gumdrops.

Charlotte and I looked at each other and smiled.

"Now the other window," said Charlotte.

We crossed in front of the doorway and gazed at the second window.

"Christmas already?" asked Charlotte, staring at a tree and Santa and presents. She looked both perplexed and dreamy. "Stacey, how long? How many days?"

"Pretty long, Char. About five weeks. The stores like to get ready early. Come on, let's go inside."

We walked through the doorway, and I was pleased to see that we weren't the only people in the little shop. Three other customers were there, and Polly and her sister were busy helping them—which meant that they were too busy to watch Charlotte and me.

The outside of Polly's Fine Candy had smelled of chocolate. The inside smelled of chocolate, and much more—ginger and cinnamon and licorice and marzipan and cream and raspberry filling and roasted nuts and raisins and cherries and spun sugar. The air was heady and warm. It was almost more than I could stand. I tried to figure out how much it would hurt to have just one piece of white chocolate.

"Look, Stacey!" Charlotte cried. She ran to a display of elaborate gingerbread houses decorated with candies and white frosting. "Oh, elves! And mice. Look at all the little creatures that live in those houses. . . . Oh!" She grabbed my hand and pulled me to the penny-candy counter. We were facing bin after bin of candy: butterscotch drops and Mary Janes and Gummi Bears and licorice sticks and peppermints. . . .

"Please, Stacey, could we get just one thing? *One* thing each?" pleaded Charlotte.

I noticed bite-size bars of white chocolate and thought I could actually *taste* one melting in my mouth.

I felt in my pocket. I had two dollars, more than enough for two pieces of candy.

"Please?"

I pulled the money out and put it on the counter. At that moment, Polly's cuckoo clock chimed. It was four-thirty. Slowly, I put the money back in my pocket and let out my breath. I couldn't believe what I'd almost done.

"Better not," I said. "It's too close to dinner. Your mom doesn't like you eating sweets anyway."

"I know," said Charlotte. "I just thought—"

"It's okay. I wanted a treat, too, but you're not the only one who's not supposed to eat sweets. Come on, let's go."

We left the store, Charlotte looking longingly over her shoulder. "Hey!" I said. "We have enough time to go to the playground before we head home."

"Goody!"

It was growing dark, but I thought we could play safely for ten minutes. I felt cheered when we reached the school and saw a group of children hanging from the monkey bars. "Come on," I said. But Charlotte had stopped in her tracks.

"No."

"It's okay. It's not dark yet. And there are other kids here."

"No. I want to go home. Let's go."

Too late. The children had spotted Charlotte.

"Hey, there's *Char*-Char," cried one.

"Hey, teacher's pet! Go away!"

"Yeah! Charlotte, Charlotte, go away, don't come back another day!"

"Teacher's pet, teacher's pet . . ."

"*I am not the teacher's pet!*" shouted Charlotte. She turned and began running home.

"Hey! Wait up! Charlotte?" I caught up with her easily.

"Go away."

"It's me, Stacey."

"I said go away."

"I can't. I'm your baby-sitter. I have to stay with you."

Charlotte marched straight ahead, chin held high, tears dripping down her cheeks.

"Did those kids tease you because they saw you with a baby-sitter? . . . Charlotte?" I tagged along at her side.

"No," she said at last, sniffling. "They don't know you're my sitter."

"Why are you mad at me?"

Charlotte stopped walking. "I'm not mad at you."

"Just upset because they teased you?"

"I guess."

"How come they teased you?"

"I don't know."

"They called you the teacher's pet."

"I don't want to talk about it."

"Hey, listen, I got teased a *lot* last year."

"In New York?"

"In New York."

"Who teased you?"

"My best friend. Well, she used to be my best friend. Now she's my former best friend."

"Why did she tease you?"

"It's a long story."

"Don't you want to talk about it, either?"

"I guess not."

We were approaching the corner of Charlotte's street. She had stopped crying and was holding my hand again. Suddenly, she squealed and pointed at something. "Look at that!"

I looked. All I could see in the dusky light was a bunch of helium balloons bobbing down the street toward us. I looked harder and realized that a person was behind them. Either that, or the balloons were propelled by a pair of legs wearing jeans and sneakers.

The balloons spoke. "Hi!"

I peered around them. Holding tightly to a handful of strings was a pretty girl, probably a couple of years older than I, tall and very thin, wearing a sweatshirt I would have died for.

She separated a red balloon from the bunch and handed it to Charlotte. Then she turned to me. "I'm Liz Lewis," she said, "president of the Baby-sitters Agency. I hope you'll call me if you ever need a sitter for your little sister." Charlotte giggled. "The number's on the balloon. Later!" She walked on.

A shiver ran down my spine, and I suddenly felt cold through and through.

Charlotte was holding the balloon in both hands. She turned it around and read slowly, "The Baby-sitters Agency. Call Liz Lewis 555-1162 or Michelle Patterson 555-7548." She looked up at me. "More baby-sitters? What's an agency, Stacey?"

"It's another long story. Come on. Let's go home."

I knew I'd be on the phone with Kristy again that evening.

CHAPTER 5

Sunday, November 23

It is almost one week since Liz Lewis and Michelle Patterson sent around their flyers. Usually, our club gets about fourteen or fifteen jobs a week. Since last Monday, we've had nine. That's why I'm writing in our notebook. This book is supposed to be a diary of our baby-sitting jobs, so each of us can write up our problems and experiences for the other club members to read. But the Baby-sitters Agency is the biggest problem we've ever had, and I plan to keep track of it in our notebook. We better do something fast.

□ □ □

Kristy was worried. She took the balloons as a personal insult. It turned out that she'd run into Liz that afternoon herself. Only Kristy had had the nerve to tell Liz who she was—president of the Baby-sitters *Club*, and therefore Liz's number one rival. According to Kristy, they had "exchanged words," which I guess meant that they had had an argument. But by the time I was talking to Kristy over the phone in the evening, all she could say was, "Why didn't *we* think of balloons? Why didn't *we* think of balloons?"

The very next day, though, Monday, something wonderful happened that took our minds off the agency—followed by something horrible that put our minds right back on it.

The Baby-sitters Club had walked home from school together. When we reached Bradford Court, Claudia went to her house to work on a painting for art class, and Mary Anne went to her house because she was supposed to bake cranberry bread for the Thanksgiving dinner she and her father would be sharing with Kristy's family (which included Watson, Kristy's stepfather-to-be, and his two little kids; Kristy said it was going to be one interesting meal).

"Want to come over for a while?" Kristy asked

me after Claudia and Mary Anne had left. (Not one of us had a baby-sitting job that afternoon.)

"Sure," I replied, eager for even a *look* at Sam Thomas.

We stepped up to her front door and Kristy took her house key out of her purse. Since her parents are divorced and Mrs. Thomas works full time, Kristy is often the first person home in the afternoon. But when she put the key in the lock, she discovered that the door was open.

"That's odd," she murmured. "I hope David Michael didn't get here first. He hates to come home to an empty house." We walked into the front hall. Kristy's mother was there.

"Mom! What are you doing home?" exclaimed Kristy.

Mrs. Thomas smiled. "Hi, honey. Hi, Stacey."

"Hi, Mrs. Thomas," I replied.

"Look who's here with me," said Kristy's mother.

"Who?" asked Kristy suspiciously.

"Come in the kitchen."

Sitting at the kitchen table was Jamie Newton. He was drinking milk and coloring in a coloring book.

"Jamie!" cried Kristy. "Hi!"

"Hi there, Jamie," I said.

"Hi-hi," answered Jamie cheerfully.

"What are you doing here?" Kristy asked him.

Jamie glanced at Kristy's mother.

"Go ahead and tell them your news, sweetie," said Mrs. Thomas.

"My mommy's having a baby," he announced. "She's at the hospital."

"Having the baby? *Now?*" asked Kristy, sounding dismayed.

"Kristy, I know you girls had plans for helping the Newtons out," her mother said, "but the baby started to come late this morning. Several weeks ago, the Newtons had asked me whether I'd be able to watch Jamie if the baby arrived at night or while you girls were in school. I told them I'd be glad to. When Mr. Newton called me at work to say that it was time for him to take his wife to the hospital, I told him just to drop Jamie by my office on the way."

"On the way!" said Kristy. "But you work in Stamford."

"I know. The Newtons' doctor is with the Stamford hospital, though, so I really was on their way. Jamie worked very hard with me today, didn't you, Jamie?"

Jamie nodded proudly.

"He made a picture for the baby and read some books and copied things on the Xerox machine."

"And we had lunch together," added Jamie.

"That's right," said Mrs. Thomas. "We ate in the cafeteria." She looked at her watch. "And now, girls," she said. "I'm leaving Jamie in your capable hands and going back to the office for a few hours."

I got the distinct impression that Mrs. Thomas hadn't gotten much work done that day.

"But, Mom, wait! What about the baby?" asked Kristy. "Don't leave us hanging!"

"Yeah!" I exclaimed. "What did Mrs. Newton have?"

"Sorry, no word yet. Mr. Newton promised he'd phone as soon as the baby is born. He knows to call here after three o'clock."

"Well, how long does it take?" asked Kristy indignantly. "I mean, to have a baby?"

Her mother smiled. "It depends on the baby. You took twenty-four hours."

"Wow," I said.

"Twenty-four hours!" cried Kristy. "Oh, no. I can*not* wait that long."

"Well, maybe this baby will come faster. Now listen, Jamie's going to stay with us until his father comes home from the hospital. Since he may be spending the night, why don't you get his pajamas and things, but stay around here the rest of the time. It'll be easier for Jamie than going back and forth. Here's the key to the Newtons' house. I'll pay you for sitting this afternoon, by the way. And I'll be home by six-thirty." Mrs. Thomas kissed Kristy good-bye and waved to Jamie and me. Then she was gone.

"Well, this isn't exactly the way I'd thought things would work out," said Kristy, "but it *is* a pretty exciting afternoon."

"I'll say! . . . Hey, where are your brothers?"

"You mean Sam?" teased Kristy.

"We-ell . . ."

"Let's see. Today's Monday so it's Charlie's day to watch David Michael. Oh, I bet he met David Michael at school and took him back to Stoneybrook High to watch cheerleading practice. Sam's probably with them."

"Cheerleading practice?"

"Yeah. David Michael loves it. He comes home and shows us the cheers."

I giggled.

"So, Jamie," said Kristy. "What do you think? You're going to be a big brother pretty soon."

Jamie shrugged and continued coloring.

"What do you want?" I asked him. "A brother or a sister?"

"Brother."

"Aren't you excited?"

Jamie shrugged again.

Kristy and I glanced at each other.

"You know," I said suddenly, not at all sure where the idea came from, "being a big brother is so important that I think you ought to have a Big Brother Party, Jamie."

Jamie looked at me with wide eyes.

Kristy jumped in immediately, understanding just what I meant. "That's right," she said. "We should celebrate this afternoon. We'll have a special Big Brother Party for our favorite big brother — you."

"A party for *me*?" said Jamie, his voice squeaking.

"Yeah, we'll invite everyone," I added. "Kristy, do you think your mother will mind?"

"Nah."

I dashed to the phone and began dialing. In ten minutes, I had spread the news to Claudia, Mary Anne, Charlotte, and the Pike kids. I'd also called a few other baby-sitting charges, but they weren't home.

"Well," I said to Kristy and Jamie when I was finished, "Claudia's on her way over, Mary Anne will come when she finishes the batter for the cranberry bread—she says she can bake it tonight—Charlotte's coming, and Mallory Pike is going to bring Claire and Margo over." (There are eight Pike kids. Mallory's ten, and Claire and Margo are four and six.)

"Terrific!" cried Kristy. She was rummaging around in the kitchen and had pulled out a bag of marshmallows, several apples, a can of juice, and a carrot, which I assumed was for me. "Claudia's bringing over something from her room," she added. "Pretzels, I think. Jamie, what would you like to do at your party? Play games?" She began to slice the apples.

Jamie nodded.

"What games?" I asked.

Jamie looked blank.

"Put some music on the stereo in the rec room and spread a bath mat on the floor," Kristy instructed me. "We can play musical rug. It's easier than musical chairs. I'll explain later."

"All right," I replied. "And we can have egg races—you know, with spoons. And the kids can make paper masks. We'll have a contest for the funniest one."

"Good idea. Then when it's time to calm everyone down, we'll see if we can get Mary Anne to read *The Little Engine That Could*. She makes it really funny, using all these different voices."

"Oh, boy!" exclaimed Jamie. "Oh, boy!"

At that moment, Claudia arrived. Charlotte was right behind her. I gave her a hug. The Pikes showed up next, and just after Mary Anne arrived, Charlie walked in with David Michael. I was so excited about the Big Brother Party that I was only a little disappointed that Sam wasn't there.

The little kids — Jamie, David Michael, Claire, and Margo — gathered excitedly in the rec room, which I had decorated hastily with a roll of green crepe paper. The members of the Baby-sitters Club looked on proudly. Mallory wandered between the two groups. But Charlotte hung back.

"Everything okay?" I asked her. She nodded shyly. "Why don't you come over here with me?" I led her to the group of kids. "This is Jamie. You know Jamie Newton, right?" Charlotte nodded again. "He's our guest of honor. He's going to become a big brother."

Jamie beamed.

"Make way for the food!" called Kristy, carrying a tray of food in from the kitchen. Charlie followed her, bringing napkins, plates, and paper cups. Then he left. I don't think Big Brother Parties held any interest for him.

"Eat now, games later!" Kristy announced.

She turned to Mary Anne and Claudia and me. "Take the food away in twenty minutes, no matter what," she whispered. "Otherwise, they're going to spoil their appetites for dinner."

Everybody helped themselves to the food. Claudia gave Jamie a paper crown to wear while he ate. When twenty minutes was up, we returned the food to the kitchen. Then the games began. Charlotte wouldn't join in musical rug or the egg races, but she did enter the mask contest. Claudia had just finished awarding prizes for the masks (we had decided that each of the kids should win a prize) when the phone rang.

"Kristy!" Charlie called from the kitchen. "Phone! It's Mr. Newton!"

"Aughh!" shrieked Kristy.

"Jamie, it's Daddy!" I cried. "Come on!"

The entire party ran into the kitchen. Charlie made a fast getaway.

Kristy grabbed up the phone. "Hello? Mr. Newton? . . . She did? . . . She *did*? Oh, that's great! It's super! . . . How much? . . . Wow. . . . Yeah, sure. Here he is." Kristy handed the phone to Jamie. "Your daddy wants to talk to you."

Jamie took the receiver and held it to his ear.

"Say hello," prompted Kristy.

"Hello. Daddy? . . . Fine. We're having a

party. . . . Okay. . . . Okay. . . . Okay. . . . Bye."

Kristy took the phone back. "When do you think you'll be home?" she asked Mr. Newton. "Oh, okay. Well, we'll give Jamie dinner. You can pick him up anytime. . . . You're welcome. And congratulations! Bye."

Kristy hung up the phone and faced us.

"What is it? What is it? What *is* it?" I cried.

"It's a—"

"Girl," supplied Jamie quietly.

We all began shrieking.

"She weighs nine pounds," added Kristy, "and her name is Lucy Jane."

More shrieking.

In the midst of the noise and excitement, I realized that Jamie was gone. I dashed out of the kitchen and checked the bathroom. No Jamie. Frantically, I ran through the first floor of the Thomases' house. I found him in the laundry room sitting next to Louie, crying.

I stepped in and sat beside him on the floor. "What's wrong, Big Brother?" I asked.

"The baby's here."

"And you wanted a boy instead of a girl, right?"

Jamie shrugged.

"Don't you like her name? I think Lucy is a pretty name."

"It's okay."

"It's a big change, huh?"

Jamie nodded.

"Your family will be different."

"Yup," said Jamie. "And that's not all."

"What do you mean?"

"Something else will be different. There will be lots of changes."

"What else will be different?" I asked.

"Kristy can't baby-sit me anymore."

"What do you mean?" That cold feeling crept into my stomach again.

"Mommy called a girl and said, 'We need an older sitter for the new baby.'"

"Was the girl named Liz Lewis?" I whispered.

"I think so. But . . . but . . ." Jamie's tears started to fall again. "I want *Kristy*!"

I pulled Jamie into my lap and sat with him for a while. Louie leaned against me and looked at us with mournful eyes.

I tried to be calm and rational. Jamie was just three years old. He had only overheard one end of a phone conversation. He wasn't even sure that Liz Lewis was the name he had overheard. Furthermore, just because Mrs. Newton had talked to someone about finding older sitters didn't mean she wasn't going to use the Baby-sitters Club anymore.

So why did I feel as if an ice chest were sitting in my stomach?

I knew why. It was because it made sense that Mrs. Newton would want someone older to take care of a newborn baby. And Liz Lewis and Michelle Patterson could provide that for her.

The Baby-sitters Club couldn't.

Still, I felt that Mrs. Newton was being a traitor. After all, Kristy was Jamie's favorite baby-sitter, and the rest of the members of our club were the Newtons' other regular sitters. We could handle caring for an infant. We were very responsible. And I was willing to bet that Liz and Michelle's sitters, even if they were in high school, weren't responsible at all. The more I thought about the Baby-sitters Agency, the angrier I felt.

Later, when the Big Brother Party was breaking up, I told Kristy what Jamie had overheard. She looked aghast. "And you know what?" I said suddenly, the anger building up inside me again.

Kristy shook her head.

"This"—I narrowed my eyes and set my jaw—"means war."

CHAPTER 6

I was all set to launch a war against the Baby-sitters Agency. So was Kristy. We were ready to let loose with every single plan or idea she had come up with. But Claudia put her foot down (so did Mary Anne), and while we were wasting time trying to decide what to do, the Baby-sitters Agency got one more step ahead of us.

The club hadn't even had a chance for a proper meeting to discuss Jamie's bad news, since Monday's meeting had been held hastily after the Big Brother Party, and Kristy and Mary Anne weren't present because they were at the Thomases', watching Jamie and cleaning up. Then on Tuesday, the very next day, the Baby-sitters Agency carried out another step in their scheme to take away our club's business. (I don't know if that's how *they* thought of what they were doing, but it's how *I* thought of it. At any rate, they were big copycats in the first place, for starting a club so much like ours and giving it a name so close to ours.)

But I'm getting off the track. On Tuesday morning, the Baby-sitters Club walked to school as a group, which was nice, because in the beginning, the club kept separating into two and two—Kristy and Mary Anne, Claudia and me. But that started to change when Kristy became a *little* interested in boys, and I wanted to have more than one close friend. Anyway, we arrived at school and guess who was there to meet us. The Baby-sitters Agency. Everywhere. Michelle and Liz were trying to recruit more sitters to call on when job requests came in.

Liz was standing on the front steps of the school, handing out her agency balloons along with flyers. Mary Anne managed to get a flyer—not from Liz but from a boy who was about to toss his in a garbage can. It was a different flyer from the one Claudia's sister had brought to us.

"Look at this," said Mary Anne. She read aloud from the flyer. "'Want to earn fast money the easy way?'"

"Fast money!" cried Kristy indignantly. "The *easy* way! Liz has no idea. Really. That girl has *no idea* what she's talking about."

"Wait, wait. Let's hear this," I said. "Go on, Mary Anne."

We were standing in a tense bunch, huddled together a few yards away from Liz. I could feel Liz's triumphant eyes on us, but I didn't give her the satisfaction of turning around.

"'Join the Baby-sitters Agency,'" Mary Anne continued. "'You do the work, but we do the hardest part of the job. Let the agency find jobs *for* you!'"

The flyer went on to explain how the agency worked, which was just about the way Kristy had guessed when she'd made her fake phone call, looking for a sitter for "Harry Kane." We had to admit that the flyers made the agency look pretty tempting. All you had to do was join—then sit back and wait for Liz or Michelle to hand you a job. Of course, you didn't get to keep all the money you earned. You had to turn some of it over to the agency (that was how Liz and Michelle made money when *they* weren't sitting), but we thought that a lot of kids would find that a small price to pay for the extra jobs they'd get through the agency.

"Boy," said Mary Anne. She scrunched up the flyer and threw it in the trash can. "The agency is probably going to have a million eighth-graders working for it."

"Yeah," said Claudia glumly, kicking a pebble with the toe of her sneaker. "For all we know, Liz and Michelle have someone recruiting sitters over at the high school, too. They could be getting twelfth-graders. I bet a senior in high school could stay out until two in the morning—or even spend the night."

"Or sit for a whole darned weekend," I said.

"But how does the agency know what kind of sitter they're giving their clients?" asked Mary Anne. "They could give someone a really irresponsible kid who just wants to make a few bucks."

"Right," said Kristy, "but why should Liz and Michelle care, as long as they get their cut of the money earned?"

We walked dejectedly into the building, carefully not looking at Liz as we went by her. I remembered something my father had said to me the year before. He'd said it when I was in the hospital after one of the times I'd gone into insulin shock in school—in the cafeteria, where absolutely *every*one had seen me fall forward into a bowl of tomato soup—and had been taken away in an ambulance. "Stacey, look at it this way, honey. The worst has happened," he'd told me. "Now things can only get better." It was a good philosophy, and I'd repeated it to myself many times since then.

"Well, you guys," I said to the members of the Baby-sitters Club as we entered the school building, "look at it this way. The worst has happened. Now things can only get better."

"Wrong," said Kristy flatly.

"What?"

"She said 'wrong,'" Claudia repeated. "Look."

We were rounding a corner. I glanced up. In the main intersection of Stoneybrook Middle School a counter had been set up. A large sign on the wall behind it screamed: THE BABY-SITTERS AGENCY, and in smaller letters: SIGN UP HERE.

Michelle Patterson and two eighth-grade girls were sitting behind the counter. Each was holding a clipboard and looked very official. A large group of girls from every grade, as well as three boys, was standing around the counter, asking questions and talking to Michelle and her helpers. I couldn't tell how many of them were signing up, but it didn't matter.

"I wonder who gave them permission to do *that*," I said.

Claudia shrugged.

"Bathroom," said Kristy urgently. We left the hall and piled into the nearest girls' room, checking to make sure the stalls were empty. Then Kristy, glaring furiously at Claudia and Mary Anne, opened her mouth to speak.

Claudia beat her to it. "Don't say it. I know what you're going to say. Okay. So we were wrong and you were right. What do you want to do about the agency? We'll do anything."

"Anything?" asked Kristy. She looked at each of us in turn.

"Anything," said Claudia.

"Ditto," said Mary Anne.

"Double ditto," I said.

"Great," said Kristy, "because I have another idea. A new one."

"Y-you do?" asked Claudia.

Kristy nodded grimly.

Claudia glanced sideways at Mary Anne.

She poked at a drop of water on a faucet. "What? I'm afraid to ask."

At that moment, the bell rang.

Kristy rolled her eyes. "No time now. I don't

care what *any* of you is doing after school. I'm calling a triple-emergency club meeting."

"Why not at recess today?" asked Mary Anne.

"Too risky," replied Kristy. "No more club business at school. For all we know, the agency has spies watching us. Anyone sitting this afternoon?"

We shook our heads. "I haven't even spoken to Dr. or Mr. Johanssen in a week," I murmured.

"I thought as much," said Kristy. "Well, today's my regular afternoon with David Michael, so we'll have to hold the meeting at my house, okay?"

"Okay," we agreed.

The meeting that afternoon was the picture of depression. The Baby-sitters Club sat around Kristy's dining room table while David Michael built a house out of wooden blocks for Louie. Kristy had served herself and Claudia and Mary Anne a snack and had poured each of us a diet soda, but the food remained untouched. We stared at our hands. Claudia shredded a paper napkin and arranged the strips in a tidy pile. Nobody spoke except Kristy.

"We can talk about my other ideas later," she said, "but the new one is to recruit more members—eighth-graders—for our club. That way we'll have some older sitters, but we won't have to copy the agency by working the way they do." She looked around the table. "Agreed?"

Claudia, Mary Anne, and I nodded silently.

The Baby-sitters Club was going to increase its numbers.

CHAPTER 7

Thanksgiving vacation was not a lot of fun that year. It came just two days after the Baby-sitters Club decided to take on new members. I didn't really mind asking other people to join our club — I figured it would be a chance to make more friends — but I didn't like the *reason* we were adding members. I was hopping mad at Liz and Michelle for hurting our club.

That was pretty much all I could think about on Thursday and Friday of Thanksgiving vacation. We had a four-day weekend, and I spent the first half of it mad at the Baby-sitters Agency.

I spent the second half of it mad at my parents.

For starters, they had said way back over the summer that we could go to New York for Thanksgiving, but the weekend before Thanksgiving they had suddenly changed their minds.

"We thought it would be nice to make our first Thanksgiving in Connecticut a true old-fashioned, New England holiday," Mom said. "I'll cook a meal that you can eat"—I scowled—"and we'll spend the day by ourselves. Dad will build a fire in the fireplace. We'll just enjoy being cozy and together in our new home."

That didn't sound so bad. In fact, I managed to enjoy our day. It even snowed a little. It was late the next day, when Mom and Dad told me the real reason for not going to New York, that I got angry at them.

They had taken me to Washington Mall, which is about half an hour away from Stoneybrook. For some reason, the day after Thanksgiving is the biggest Christmas shopping day of the season. I don't know why. But I love to shop, so I thought the excursion would be fun and would help take my mind off the Baby-sitters Agency. Kristy had told me all about Washington Mall. It's the biggest one around, with five levels of stores, a zillion restaurants and food stands, four movie theaters, a videogame arcade, a petting zoo, and an exhibits area.

I had taken some of the money I'd earned baby-sitting out of my savings account, and I left Mom and Dad to explore the mall on my own. I bought two Christmas presents—a pair of striped leg warmers for Claudia and a book about New York for Mary Anne—and a dinosaur pin for me. I planned to attach it to my beret.

At one o'clock, I met Mom and Dad and we ate lunch in a sandwich shop. After lunch, we went to a movie. Two hours later, as we filed back into the mall, Dad said brightly, "Well, how about one more treat before we head home? We could go to that little French café on the top level."

"Ooh, goody," I said.

When we were settled, Dad with a cup of coffee, Mom with a glass of wine, and I with diet ginger ale, Dad glanced at Mom and said, "Now, honey?"

"What?" I asked, immediately suspicious.

"We have some news for you."

"What is it?"

Mom and Dad kept looking at each other as if they couldn't decide who should tell me the news. I knew it must be pretty important. Furthermore, I had a feeling that whatever it was, I wasn't going to like it one bit.

"We aren't moving again, are we?" I asked.

"Heavens, no," said Mom. "It's not bad news . . . exactly."

"You're pregnant!" I cried. "You found out you can have a baby after all!"

"Shhh!" said Dad. "People are turning around."

"Well, *what*?"

70

Mom cleared her throat. "It's just that we've scheduled the tests with the new doctor I mentioned to you a couple of weeks ago, remember?"

"How could I forget?"

"Stacey," said Dad warningly, his voice rising on the last syllable.

"Sorry."

"They're going to be a little later in the month than we had thought."

"Near *Christ*mas?" I asked, dismayed.

"We'll leave on Friday, the twelfth, and probably return on Wednesday, the seventeenth."

"But—but that's five days!" I sputtered. "You said it would only be three days."

"Well, you'll still miss just three days of school," said my father. "When we found out the tests would take longer than we realized, we scheduled them over a weekend. That's why we didn't go to New York for Thanksgiving. Two long weekends there so close together are too many."

"Am I going to be in the *hospital* for five days?" Being in the hospital when you feel fine has to be the most boring thing in the world.

"You'll spend a lot of time at this doctor's clinic," replied Mom, "but you'll be an outpatient. . . . Look, in the evenings we can have fun. And we'll have Sunday free. We can visit your cousins and go Christmas shopping—"

"And," said Dad, grinning, "I got tickets to the Sunday performance of *Paris Magic*."

"*Paris Magic*!" I cried, momentarily forgetting doctors and clinics. "You're kidding! I can't believe it! Oh, thank you!" *Paris Magic* was a musical I'd been dying to see.

"And we'll go to Rockefeller Center and look at the Christmas tree," Mom went on. "Think of it, Stacey. Christmas in New York. You always liked the city best at that season."

"I guess," I replied, returning to earth. Tickets to *Paris Magic* didn't make up for what Mom and Dad were doing to me. "So what does Dr. Werner think of . . . what's the name of the new doctor?"

"Dr. Barnes," said Dad.

"What does Dr. Werner think of Dr. Barnes?"

"She doesn't know about Dr. Barnes yet," replied my mother.

"Mo-*om*, I'd like to check with Dr. Werner first."

"Stacey," said Dad. "You are not in charge here. Your mother and I make the decisions."

"Decisions about *me*, *my* body."

"That's what parents are for," he said wryly.

"So what's so special about Dr. Barnes?" I asked. "Why do we have to see him . . . or her?"

"Him," said Mom. "He's a holistic doctor."

Holistic . . . holy? "A *faith* healer?" I squeaked. "You're taking me to a religious person for a miracle?" Mom and Dad had considered some pretty desperate things over the months, but nothing like faith healing.

"Stacey, for pity's sake. *No*," said Dad. "Calm down. Holistic medicine deals with the whole body, with a person as a whole, made up not just of physical parts, but of mental, emotional, environmental, nutritional—"

"I get it, I get it," I muttered, embarrassed.

Dad drained his coffee, Mom sipped her wine, and I stirred my soda with the straw.

"Well," said Dad at last, "we just wanted you to know what to expect. And to keep those days open for our trip."

"What about my schoolwork?" I asked.

"We'll talk to your teachers before we leave. Maybe you can bring some of your homework with you and do it at the clinic," said Mom. "Then you won't be too far behind when we return."

I nodded. "I think this is very unfair," I said softly.

My parents sighed in unison. "Well, we're sorry, honey," replied Mom. "But this is the way things are."

□ □ □

On Saturday afternoon, I baby-sat for Charlotte Johanssen. It was my first job in over a week. I knew that her parents were using the agency in the evenings because then they didn't have to worry about being home early. I hadn't seen Charlotte since the Big Brother Party. I brought the Kid-Kit with me as I had promised, and we began reading *The Cricket in Times Square*.

When the Johanssens came home, I waited until Dr. Johanssen had paid me before I finally asked, "Could I talk to you? Please?"

"Of course, Stacey," Charlotte's mother replied. "Let's go in the den."

We walked across the hall and Dr. Johanssen closed the door behind us. "What's up? Are you feeling all right?" she asked.

"That's just the trouble. I'm fine. But Mom and Dad want me to see another new doctor in New York. He's going to do all these tests at his clinic. We have to go away for *five days*."

Dr. Johanssen shook her head in sympathy.

"He's a holistic doctor. Dad explained what that means." I giggled. "I thought it meant he was holy—a faith healer."

Charlotte's mother didn't smile, though. She

looked at me sharply. "Holistic. A clinic? Do you know the doctor's name?"

"Dr. Barnes."

Dr. Johanssen groaned. "You weren't too far wrong, Stacey. Dr. Barnes *calls* himself a holistic doctor but he practically *is* a faith healer. At any rate, I don't think he's much more than a quack. He just happens to be getting a lot of publicity now. He's a fad doctor. And he's giving good holistic doctors a bad reputation. I don't know him personally," she added, "I've just heard about him."

"I knew it, I knew it," I moaned.

"Now, don't worry. Dr. Barnes isn't going to harm you, from what I've heard. He won't touch your insulin, and if he changes your diet, it will be only slightly. What he is going to do—I can practically guarantee this—is recommend all sorts of expensive programs and therapies designed to make your life as positive and fulfilling and healthy as possible. He'll tell your parents that this will enable you to rid your body of the disease."

"What kinds of therapies?" I asked.

"Oh, everything. He'll tell your parents to send you to a psychologist or psychiatrist. He'll give you an exercise program, start you on recreational therapy. He may even recommend that you change schools so you can get individualized instruction."

"No!" I cried.

"There's nothing really wrong with any of those things. It's just that—well, it's my belief that no special program is going to rid your body of diabetes."

I stood up. "Of course not! Are they crazy? How is a psychiatrist going to change my blood sugar? Dr. Johanssen, you have to help me. Help me get out of this."

"Stacey, I'd like to, but I don't feel I can step in here. I barely know your parents."

"But you know me, and you're a doctor."

"Yes, but I'm not *your* doctor."

"Please?"

Dr. Johanssen rose, too. She put her arm around me. "Let me think, hon. I can't intervene directly, but before you leave for New York I'll—" She paused. "I promise I won't let you go to New York without doing *some*thing. I just need to think. Fair enough?"

I nodded. "Thanks."

On my way home that afternoon, I vowed that I would not let Dr. Barnes put me on any of his programs. But I had only two weeks to figure out how to stop him.

CHAPTER 8

For years, my parents have watched me go off to school wearing unusual clothing and accessories. They've let all sorts of things go by them unmentioned: the dinosaur on my beret, red sneakers covered with beads and glitter, leg warmers covered with footprints, plastic butterflies in my hair. For two weeks in New York I even wore red lace gloves with no fingertips.

But they'd never seen anything quite like what Kristy made the members of the Baby-sitters Club wear to school the Monday after Thanksgiving vacation. Even I was embarrassed. And poor Mary Anne looked as if she'd rather be stranded on a desert island with no hope of rescue.

Kristy had been busy during vacation. She'd made each of us a sandwich board to wear to school. The part that went over our fronts said JOIN THE BEST CLUB AROUND. The part that went over our backs said, in the block design Claudia had thought up for our flyers: THE BABY-SITTERS CLUB.

"Put these on," said Kristy when we met on the street in front of my house. She was already wearing hers.

"Now?" I asked.

Kristy nodded. "We're going to look for new club members today and we might as well start on the way to school. Plenty of kids will see us."

"That's what I'm afraid of," whispered Claudia.

I shrugged. Then I put my notebook down. "Well, I'm ready."

Kristy helped me fit one of the ad boards over my head. I adjusted the strings on my shoulders. Then we helped Claudia and Mary Anne with theirs. Mary Anne's cheeks were burning bright red.

"Okay, let's go," I said. I waved self-consciously to my parents, who were standing at the front door.

We marched off to Stoneybrook Middle School. All along the way, kids stopped and stared.

"I hope I don't see Trevor," Claudia murmured to me.

Trevor Sandbourne is Claudia's boyfriend. Sort of. He had taken Claudia to the Halloween

Hop, and once they had gone to the movies. I could understand why she didn't want Trevor to see her.

"I know," I replied. "I hope we don't see Pete. Or Sam."

"Oh, no. Oh, *no*!" Claudia suddenly cried.

"What? Is it Trevor? Pete?"

"No. Look." Claudia pointed down the road behind us.

I turned around. A school bus was heading our way, loaded with high school students. They hung out of the windows and called to us as the bus passed by.

"Hey, hey!"

"Whoooo! The Baby-sitters Club!"

"Hey, girls, give me your number! *I* might need a sitter!"

Kristy held her head high and kept walking, looking straight ahead.

"I'm dying, I'm dying," I whispered to Claudia. But I told myself that if I felt like a fool, it was for the sake of the club. And the club was worth it.

We reached school fifteen minutes before the first bell.

"Okay, now spread out," Kristy instructed.

"You mean we have to do this *alone*?" cried Mary Anne.

Kristy nodded. "Yes," she said firmly. "Walk around outside the building where kids can see you as they arrive at school. If anyone asks you questions, tell them about the club. Make sure they know they get to keep all the money they earn. And especially try to get some eighth-graders interested. Tell them the first meeting they'll attend will be on Wednesday."

We separated then, and I wandered around by the main entrance to the school. Every single kid stared at me as he or she went by. Some pointed at the sign, then turned to speak to friends. A few laughed at me. But only three kids asked any questions.

"What's the Baby-sitters Club?" each one wanted to know. I explained. I even told them about some of the kids we sat for.

"You ought to meet Charlotte Johanssen," I said to one girl (who, unfortunately, was a sixth-grader). "She's such a great little kid. She loves to be read to."

"You *read* to her?" said the girl incredulously. "Gosh, when I baby-sit, I use the time to watch TV."

"You do?" I said, just as incredulously. "What do the kids do while you're watching? Watch with you?"

She shrugged. "Sometimes. . . . I don't really care."

"Oh. . . ." She was not right for our club. I was glad she didn't ask any more questions.

The second kid, a boy, said, "You have to go to three meetings a week? I don't think I could fit that into—into my schedule."

The third kid was an eighth-grade girl who hated Liz Lewis. Perfect!

I told her about Charlotte.

I told her about David Michael.

I told her about Jamie.

I told her about Claire and Margo Pike and Nina and Eleanor Marshall. Then I told her about the meetings and the notebook. "It sounds like too much work," she said, and left.

The bell rang. The Baby-sitters Club walked into school together—Claudia, Mary Anne, and I—taking our sandwich boards off as we went.

Kristy was grinning. "How did you guys do?" she asked.

"Terrible," I muttered.

"Rotten," said Claudia.

"Awful," said Mary Anne. "How come you're smiling?"

"Because I have good news!" announced

Kristy. "But we won't discuss it in school. I'll tell you everything at our meeting this afternoon. . . . And put your signs back on. Wear them in the halls and the cafeteria today."

"In the cafeteria! How are we supposed to eat with these things on?" asked Claudia crossly. "We can't sit down."

"Well, at least wear them in the lunch line."

"Oh, fine," grumbled Claudia, but she joined Mary Anne and me in placing the signs back over our shoulders.

I went to my locker, put my lunch away, and got out the books I'd need for the morning. Then I rushed off to English class. On the way, I passed Pete Black.

I nearly fainted.

Between math class and advanced French (I was in the advanced class because in my school in New York we had been given French lessons since kindergarten), I passed Pete again.

He didn't look at me. Had he really not seen me, or was he embarrassed by the sign?

It didn't matter, because at lunchtime, when I approached our table in the cafeteria, still bravely wearing the sign, Pete looked up and smiled at me. "Let me help you take that thing off," he said. He lifted it over my shoulders.

"Embarrassed to be seen with me while I'm wearing it?" I asked.

Pete grinned. "Nah. . . . Well, maybe a little. But it takes guts to do what you're doing."

"Want to be in the club? We could use some boys."

Pete coughed. "*Me?* Take care of little kids?"

"Sure, why not?"

"I—I wouldn't know what to do."

"Well, never mind. It's okay."

We turned to our lunches. Pete is very serious about food. We'd been eating for about five minutes when I noticed that his face was turning red.

"Hey, what's wrong? Are you all right?" I thought he might be choking.

Pete swallowed. "Yeah, sure. I'm fine. But I have to ask you something."

"Okay."

"What I was wondering is . . . do you want to go to the Snowflake Dance with me?"

"That's not until December, is it?"

"This is December. It's December first."

"Oh, wow! You're right." I was really flattered. Even if it was December, the dance was still almost three weeks away. And Pete was already asking me. "I'd love to go," I told him. "Thanks."

Across the table, Claudia was grinning at me. Suddenly, I knew I wouldn't mind wearing the sandwich board anymore.

Kristy was in a great mood at our meeting that afternoon. I couldn't see why. "*No*body wanted to join the club," I told her. I was lounging on Claudia's bed, my feet propped up on the headboard. "It seems to be too much work."

"Yeah," said Claudia, who was sitting next to me. She rummaged around in her pillowcase, trying to find some candy she'd hidden there.

"Yeah," agreed Mary Anne from her spot in the director's chair.

"But *I* got two new members," Kristy told us proudly. "And they're both eighth-graders."

"You're kidding!" I exclaimed. "That's super!"

"What are their names?" asked Claudia.

"Janet Gates and Leslie Howard."

Claudia frowned. "I thought they were friends of Liz's," she said slowly.

Kristy looked smug. "Not anymore. They were part of the agency, but they dropped out. They didn't like it."

"Defectors," I said.

"Already?" asked Mary Anne.

"Yup," replied Kristy.

"Gosh, the agency must be pretty bad if kids are dropping out so soon," I said.

"Leslie said they didn't like having to give Liz and Michelle part of what they earned. Plus, Liz gave them really horrible kids to sit for. She kept all the nice, well-behaved ones for herself and Michelle."

"So they're coming to the next meeting?" asked Claudia.

"Yeah."

"But . . . something's wrong about this," said Mary Anne. "Something . . . I know what it is. Remember when we were first starting the club and we were deciding whether to invite Stacey to join? We didn't know her, so we asked her all sorts of things about the baby-sitting she did in New York. We wanted a club of *good* baby-sitters. Dedicated baby-sitters. Do you know anything about Janet and Leslie, Kristy?"

"Well, no," she admitted.

"And you've already told them they can be members?"

"Yes. . . ."

"Gosh, I don't know."

"It seems risky," I said.

Kristy looked at us uncomfortably. "Well,

it's too late now. We'll just have to take our chances."

Claudia found several pieces of candy in her pillowcase and handed them to Kristy and Mary Anne. They unwrapped them and began crunching away.

"Well, there's one good thing," I spoke up.

"What?" everybody asked eagerly.

"If the agency is as horrible as Janet and Leslie say, maybe it won't last long."

"Yeah," agreed the others.

We sat quietly, and after a moment I realized that the four of us were staring at the phone. "I wonder if we could make it ring if we all concentrated on it," I said. We tried, but nothing happened.

At six o'clock, when the meeting ended, we hadn't gotten a single Baby-sitters Club call.

CHAPTER 9

The next afternoon, since none of us had a baby-sitting job and we were very bored, we went over to the Thomases' house. Kristy called Mrs. Newton, who was home from the hospital, and asked if we could visit them and see the new baby. When she said yes, we were really excited.

"Oh, goody!" exclaimed Kristy after she'd hung up the phone. "I have a present for the baby, and one for Jamie, too."

"So do I," I said.

"So do I," said Claudia.

"So do I," said Mary Anne.

"Are they wrapped?" asked Claudia.

"No," we answered.

"Good. Go get your presents and meet me in my room. I've got great stuff for gift wrapping."

When we were gathered in Claudia's room, we spread out our presents. We all began to squeal, "Oh, that's so *cute*!"

Kristy had gotten a little toy car for Jamie and a rattle shaped like a duck for Lucy. Claudia had bought Jamie a dinosaur and had painted a picture of kittens for Mrs. Newton to hang in the baby's room. I had bought two books: a paperback called *Mike Mulligan and His Steam Shovel* for Jamie and *Pat the Bunny* for Lucy.

Mary Anne's gifts were the best of all: a red ski hat for Jamie and a little pink hat for the baby.

"I made them," she said shyly. "Can you tell?"

"You're kidding!" I exclaimed. "You *made* those?"

"Then you couldn't tell?"

"No way!"

"Mary Anne, I didn't know you could knit," said Kristy.

Mary Anne glanced at Claudia, who smiled at her.

"Mimi's teaching her," said Claudia. "She's been dying to teach someone, but Janine and I aren't interested."

"She remembers my mother," added Mary Anne. "She tells me about her while I work."

"That's—that's great," I said. (Was that what I was supposed to say?)

Mary Anne brightened. "She's going to help me make a scarf for my father."

"Wow!" We were all impressed.

Claudia hauled a big square carton out of her closet. "Okay, go to town," she said.

We looked in the box. It was jammed with stuff Claudia had collected over the years: plastic flowers, papers hearts, beads, bows, ribbons, felt animals. "Those are package decorations," she told us. "We can make our own wrapping paper with these." She opened a shoe box that was full of rubber stamps. "See? I've got four ink pads in different colors. You can stamp this white paper to make any design you want. Then we'll decorate the packages with the other stuff."

We got right to work. I printed red hearts and blue flowers on Lucy's paper, and big green frogs saying "Ribbit!" on Jamie's paper. When we were finished, we admired our packages briefly, and then ran to the Newtons' house.

Jamie answered the door. "Hi-hi," he greeted us.

Mrs. Newton appeared behind him. "Hello, there! Oh, I'm so glad to see you! Jamie has missed you, and I'm dying for you to meet Lucy. Come on inside."

We stepped through the door. I was surprised to see that Mrs. Newton still looked, well, fat. Not pregnant exactly, but not the way I'd thought she would look after the baby was born.

"Oh, you girls are so sweet. You've brought gifts. You didn't have to do that."

"We know," said Kristy, grinning.

"We just wanted to," I added.

"Yeah," said Mary Anne. "Babies are special."

Jamie eyed the presents, then glanced at his mother. "Are any of those for me?"

"Jamie! It's not polite to ask!" Mrs. Newton turned to us. "I'm sorry. The last week has been difficult. Jamie is a bit J-E-A-L-O-U-S," she spelled. "L-U-C-Y has been given a lot of P-R-E-S-E-N-T-S."

"Well, you're in luck, Jamie," said Claudia. "Four of these are for you."

"Four!" cried Jamie.

We didn't make him wait. We handed him his presents and he tore into them. "What do you say?" prompted Mrs. Newton.

"Thank you," replied Jamie automatically. He was wearing the hat and trying to read the book and play with the toys at the same time.

Then we gave Mrs. Newton Lucy's gifts.

"Let's go peek at the baby before I open them," she said. "I wish Lucy was awake so you could hold her, but she's still napping."

She led us upstairs and into the little room that had been fixed up for Lucy. A big white crib stood in one corner, but Lucy was asleep in a blue bassinet near the door. "She's too little for the crib," Mrs. Newton whispered. "Infants feel more secure in a small bed."

The members of the Baby-sitters Club silently surrounded the bassinet and peered inside.

"Ohhh," I breathed.

"She's so *little*," whispered Mary Anne.

She certainly was. I guess I hadn't realized just how little a newborn baby really is.

"Can I touch her?" I asked Mrs. Newton softly.

She nodded.

I leaned over and ran my finger along one of Lucy's tiny hands. It was soft as silk, and perfect: four little fingers and a thumb, each ending in a fingernail no bigger than a speck. I breathed in. Lucy smelled sweet, like baby powder and milk. I ran my hand lightly over the fine dark hair on her head. She stirred then and opened her eyes just long enough for me to see that they were a deep blue. Then she closed them again.

I glanced up. Claudia, Kristy, and Mary Anne looked enchanted.

A few moments later, we were back downstairs, sitting in the living room, while Mrs. Newton opened the baby presents. She exclaimed over each one and commented on the original wrapping.

"Do you think the hat will fit?" Mary Anne asked anxiously.

"In a few weeks it should be just right."

Mary Anne let out a sigh of relief.

"Mrs. Newton?" Kristy said. "Could I ask you something?"

"Of course."

Suddenly, my stomach lurched. I had this horrible feeling I knew what Kristy was going to ask. I looked over at Claudia and found that she was already looking at me. Oh, no, her eyes seemed to be saying, I can't believe she's going to bring this up *now*.

But she did.

"I'm not sure how to say this," Kristy began, "but when Jamie was at our house last week, he said we wouldn't be baby-sitting for him anymore. I mean, no—He said he heard you on the phone with Liz Lewis from the Baby-sitters Agency. Is—? Can we still—?" Kristy didn't know how to finish what she had started.

Mrs. Newton's face was flushed with embarrassment. I was pretty sure mine was, too. It felt very hot.

"I guess I should have told you," said Mrs. Newton. "I knew how excited you were about the new baby. And of course you'll always be our favorite sitters. It's just that an infant is so delicate and fragile, and needs extra-special care—"

"But we're responsible," protested Kristy.

"I've taken care of babies before," I added.

"Newborns?" asked Mrs. Newton.

"Well, one was ten months and the other was eight months."

"That makes a big difference," she said. "There's even a big difference between a three-month-old baby and a newborn. Anyway, what I was going to say is that for the next few months, I'll simply feel more comfortable leaving Lucy with an older sitter. The times when I take Lucy with me and there's just Jamie to sit for, I'll be glad to use the Baby-sitters Club."

"I can understand that," Claudia said slowly.

"I'm glad you still want us to sit for Jamie," said Kristy.

"And when Lucy is older, I hope you'll be my regular sitters again," added Mrs. Newton.

"Oh, definitely!" I said, but I didn't feel nearly as cheerful as I sounded. Nothing seemed to be going our way anymore.

□ □ □

After school the next day, I met Janet and Leslie for the first time. They arrived promptly at five-thirty for our Wednesday meeting of the Baby-sitters Club.

I studied them critically. Of course, they were already members of the club, but I couldn't resist asking them a few questions.

"Have you done a lot of baby-sitting?" I asked Janet.

"Oh, tons," she replied. She was chewing a wad of gum and she cracked it loudly.

"You, too?" I asked Leslie.

Leslie looked bored. She brushed her shaggy hair out of her face. I noticed that she was wearing makeup. A lot of it.

"Sure," she replied. She glanced at Janet, and they exchanged tiny smiles.

"Where?" asked Mary Anne. I was surprised to see her jumping in, but I knew she was concerned about our reputation.

"Over on the other side of town," replied Janet. (*Crack, crack. Snap.*) "You probably wouldn't know any of the people."

"How old's the youngest kid you ever sat for?" asked Claudia.

"About nine months," said Leslie.

"Same (*crack*) here," said Janet.

Kristy was watching us nervously, her eyes traveling back and forth between the new members of the club and the old members.

"How many kids can you sit for at one time?" I wanted to know.

"Oh, three or four, I guess," answered Leslie.

"Yeah," said Janet. (*Crack, snap.*)

Kristy must have decided it was time to impress us. "How late can you stay out?" she asked.

"Eleven o'clock on weekdays," they replied at the same time.

"On Friday and Saturday nights (*crack*) I can stay out until midnight (*snap*)," added Janet.

"I can stay out until any hour on the weekend as long as I tell my mom first," said Leslie.

My jaw dropped open. "How old are you?"

"Fourteen," she replied.

"I'm thirteen," said Janet.

I began to feel the tiniest bit impressed.

Kristy looked around triumphantly. "I think what we ought to do now is let our clients know about our new members." She pulled a copy of our old Baby-sitters Club flyer out of a folder she was carrying. "We'll add Janet's and Leslie's names and ages to this, and the times when we can sit. Then we'll print out the new version of the flyer and distribute the copies as soon as possible. Who can help me tomorrow after school?"

"I can," said Claudia, Mary Anne, and I.

We looked at Janet and Leslie. They were looking at each other.

"Well," said Janet (*crackle, crackle*), "we'd like to help you, but we have baby-sitting jobs tomorrow (*crack*). You know, previous commitments."

Kristy glanced at me as if to say, See how responsible they are?

"All right," said Kristy. "Here's the plan of action. Tomorrow, we distribute flyers. We'll also call our best customers personally to tell them the news. Friday, we meet again."

We followed Kristy's plan. And at the Friday meeting, we got four baby-sitting jobs. Two were last-minute late-night ones for Janet and Leslie over the weekend. We couldn't wait for our Monday meeting to see how things had gone.

The Baby-sitters Club seemed to be back on its feet.

CHAPTER 10

Monday, December 8

Today Kristy, Stacey & Mary Anne all arrived early for our Baby-Sitters Club meeting. We were all realy excited to find out how Janet and Leslie's siting jobs had gone on Saturday. When it was 5:30 we kept expecting the doorbell to ring any second. But it didn't. Soon it was 5:50. Where were they? Kristy was getting worried. Write this down in our notebook, somebody, she said. Something's wrong. Unfortunately, Kristy was right. It turned out that something was very very wrong. And it was part of the awful thing with the Baby-sitters Agency.

□ □ □

Wow. What happened on Monday was one of the worst events in the war between the Baby-sitters Club and the Baby-sitters Agency. As Claudia mentioned, the four original club members gathered early for our Monday meeting. We couldn't wait to talk to Janet and Leslie.

Despite the fact that Claudia's digital clock flipped to 5:35 and the new members hadn't shown up yet, the meeting got off to a good start. First, Mrs. Marshall called, needing a sitter for Wednesday afternoon. Mary Anne took the job. Then Watson, Kristy's future stepfather, needed a sitter for an early evening job on Wednesday. Kristy took that one, of course. Then Mrs. Newton called! She wanted someone to watch Jamie on Wednesday afternoon while she took Lucy to the pediatrician for a checkup. I took that job, since Claudia has art lessons on Wednesdays. We were so busy taking calls that it was 5:50 before we looked at the clock again and realized Janet and Leslie were late.

"They could have at least called to say they weren't going to make the meeting this afternoon," I pointed out.

Even Kristy looked miffed. "I saw Janet in school today, and she didn't say anything about not coming."

"I think it's weird that *neither* of them showed up," said Mary Anne. "What could have happened to make them both late?"

Kristy shrugged. "Maybe they just forgot."

"We've told them about meetings a million times," said Claudia. "If they forgot, then they're pretty irresponsible."

"Well, I'll call them," said Kristy. She knew something was wrong then, because that was when she told Claudia to write about the incident in our notebook.

"No, I'll call them," I said. "I want to know who they think they are!"

"Don't get mad," said Kristy. "It won't help. *I'll call*. I'm the president."

"No, *I* want to c—"

The phone rang then. Kristy and I both lunged for it, but Mary Anne was sitting practically on top of it. She beat us to it.

"Hello, the Baby-sitters Club," she said. "... No, this is Mary Anne Spier. Can I help you? ... Oh, hi, Mr. Kelly. . . . She *didn't?*"

Kristy and Claudia and I jerked to attention. The Kellys were the new family Leslie had arranged to sit for on Saturday night. They had contacted the club after we'd sent around our updated flyers.

"Mr. Kelly," Mary Anne was saying, "I'm terribly sorry. I don't know what happened. . . . Well, I'd like to, but she's not here right now. I guess you could call her at home. . . . Oh, I see. Well, would you like to speak to our president? . . . Okay. . . . Sure. And I—I'm really sorry."

Mary Anne's face was flaming. She cupped her hand over the mouthpiece, and as she passed the receiver to Kristy, she whispered, "Leslie never showed up on Saturday. She didn't even bother to call the Kellys."

Kristy took the phone, her eyes closed, steeling herself for the conversation with Mr. Kelly. "Kristy Thomas here," she said after a moment, "club president. . . . Yes, Mary Anne just mentioned that. I feel terrible. Leslie never told *me* she wasn't going to be able to keep her appointment with you. If she had, I would have sent over one of our other fine sitters. . . . I hope you can accept our apologies. . . . Sure. . . . Sure. Okay, goodbye."

Kristy hung up the phone. I couldn't tell whether she was angry or scared or embarrassed. Maybe she was all three. She kept still for so long that at last I said, "He was really mad, right?"

"Yup. He and his wife had tickets to see his wife's brother perform in a concert in Stamford.

When Leslie didn't show up, he called her house, but no one was home. The Kellys had to scramble around trying to get someone to watch their kids. At last, they left them with a neighbor, but by the time they reached the concert hall, they'd missed twenty minutes of the concert."

"Uh-oh," said Claudia.

"Why didn't they just call one of us?" I asked.

"Simple," snapped Kristy. "They didn't trust us, and why should they? Mr. Kelly was only calling now to make sure we knew what Leslie had done. I have a feeling the Kellys won't be calling the Baby-sitters Club again."

"Oh, great," I said, letting out a breath I hadn't even realized I'd been holding. "Wait'll word gets around about *this*."

The phone rang again. Nobody made a move to answer it. Finally, I picked it up on the third ring. "Hello, the Baby-sitters Club," I said glumly. "Stacey McGill speaking. . . . Yes? . . . Oh, no, you're *kid*ding! I mean, I'm sorry, I'm so sorry. We had no idea. Maybe you'd like to talk to our president. . . . Okay, hold on." I handed Kristy the phone, whispering, "I don't believe it. This is Ms. Jaydell. You know, the other new client? The woman *Janet* was supposed to sit for? Janet didn't show up, either."

It was Kristy's turn to be furious. She jerked the phone to her ear, eyes flashing, and had to unclench her jaw before saying (fairly civilly), "Kristin Thomas speaking."

I'd seen Kristy mad before, but never *that* mad.

She carried on pretty much the same conversation with Ms. Jaydell that she'd had with Mr. Kelly a few minutes earlier. The only difference was that Ms. Jaydell and her husband hadn't been able to find another sitter and had missed out on a cocktail party.

When Kristy hung up the phone, she burst into tears. It was the first time I'd ever seen her cry.

"Well, that does it," I said, handing her a tissue from the table by Claudia's bed. "What're Janet's and Leslie's phone numbers? I'm going to call them right now. They're really hurting us."

"No," said Kristy, wiping her eyes. "Don't call them. I want to confront them face-to-face. We'll talk to them in school tomorrow. This wasn't any accident. They missed those jobs on purpose. I'm sure of it."

"But why?" asked Claudia.

"Beats me," said Kristy. "Who's going to help me face those traitors tomorrow?"

"I am!" I said.

"I am!" said Claudia.

We looked at Mary Anne. "Couldn't we confront them over the phone?" she asked.

"Over the phone is not a confrontation," I said firmly.

"We have to be face-to-face."

"We do?"

"Yes, we do."

"*All* of us," added Kristy. "The whole club. United."

"All right," said Mary Anne at last.

None of us was looking forward to school the next day. We walked together in the morning, traveling about as fast as snails.

"When are we going to confront them?" I asked Kristy as we reached Stoneybrook Middle School.

"Yeah," said Claudia. "We don't have any classes with them."

"We're going to confront them right now," Kristy replied. "I know where their homerooms are. We're going to wait for them."

"An ambush," said Mary Anne.

Janet and Leslie were not in the same homeroom, but the rooms were just across the hall from each other. Kristy and Mary Anne waited by Janet's room; Claudia and I waited by Leslie's.

After about five minutes of standing around, I spotted them down the hall. "Psst! Kristy!" I said. "Here they come. Both of them."

"Hey," Claudia whispered to me. "Look who's with them."

I looked. It was Liz Lewis. "I thought they didn't like Liz," I said.

"I know." Claudia frowned.

We watched the girls stop for a moment, talking earnestly. Then Liz waved to them and disappeared into a classroom.

Janet and Leslie saw us before they reached their homerooms. They nudged each other, laughing.

The members of the Baby-sitters Club converged on them.

"Where were you yesterday?" Kristy demanded.

"Hey (*snap, snap*), what kind of a greeting is that?" asked Janet. She must have had twelve pieces of gum in her mouth.

"I'm not kidding," said Kristy. "I want to know where you were, and I want to know why you didn't show up for your Saturday sitting jobs. Our club is known for responsible baby-sitters."

"So what?" said Leslie.

"So what!" exclaimed Kristy. "You're giving us a bad reputation. We're going to have to ask you to leave the club."

"Fine with us," replied Janet. "We," she added with a smirk, "are members of the Baby-sitters *Agency.*" She and Leslie burst into hysterical laughter.

"But—but—" stammered Kristy.

"We had you completely fooled!"

"You're rats!" I cried suddenly. "Both of you. You did this to make us look bad! That's—it's—it's *dirty.* It's not fair."

Janet and Leslie couldn't stop laughing. And I couldn't stop accusing. "You're liars! And—and dirty businesswomen!"

"Whoa," said Leslie. "Get that. Dirty business-women. Pretty high-class talk."

"And probably *rotten* baby-sitters," Kristy added.

Leslie took some offense at that. "We are *not* rotten baby-sitters," she said, bristling.

"Well, what do you call a baby-sitter who doesn't show up for a job and doesn't call the parents to explain why?"

"Hmm," said Leslie. "Janet, what would you call that sitter?"

"I'd call her anything except late for dinner!"

Leslie and Janet doubled over with laughter at their stupid joke.

"Shut up! Shut up!" cried Kristy. "I hope you realize you're in big trouble."

"With who?" said Janet, still laughing.

"With . . . with the parents. I'm going to call them and tell them exactly what happened. Then they'll call their friends, and their friends will call *their* friends. Word will get around. You'll be sorry."

At last, the girls stopped laughing. "You wouldn't dare," said Janet, at the same time that Leslie said, "No, *you'll* be sorry, tattletale."

"Me? Why should I be sorry?" asked Kristy.

"Because," replied Leslie, "Liz and Michelle will be interested in your plans. They'll just have to work a little harder to be the best sitting agency in town. But they won't mind that."

"You—" exclaimed Kristy, simmering "— you are *pigs*!"

Janet snapped her gum. "Sorry, *kids*." She and Leslie separated and walked into their classrooms.

Kristy, Claudia, Mary Anne, and I were left standing in the hall. For the second time in two days, Kristy began to cry. The rest of us surrounded her and walked her into the nearest girls' room. It was pretty crowded, but we huddled in a corner and no one paid much attention to us.

"I'm so embarrassed," Kristy wailed. "It *isn't* fair. That was a really rotten trick. Besides, a baby-sitting club was *my* idea, not Liz's. We worked *so hard* on our club. And even when the agency started up, we never tried to hurt them. We just tried to protect what we had." She blew her nose on a paper towel. "Now they're purposely trying to beat us out."

"So Liz put Janet and Leslie up to what they did," I said slowly.

Kristy nodded. "Yes. And it's all my fault for being so stupid about taking on new members. Mary Anne was right. I should have checked on them."

"Well," said Claudia, "I agree that what the agency is doing to us is really mean. But I think what we have to do is just keep going—the four of us. Okay, so we can't stay out late. So we're only twelve years old. Most of our clients like us a lot. We'll just go on being as responsible and good with children and—and—what's that word that means you sort of adjust yourself to whatever people need?"

"Flexible?" suggested Mary Anne.

"Almost," Claudia replied. "That's not the word, but it's close."

"I know what you mean," said Kristy. "I guess you're right. Anyway, I *am* going to explain things to Mr. Kelly and Ms. Jaydell."

"And," I added frantically, "there's always lower rates and housework and special deals."

"No," said Kristy. "I've decided that's not the way to go. The club will survive, but we don't want to become butlers. Besides, I can't deal with any of that stuff right now. We've got to think of ways to prove that *we're* better than the agency."

With that, the bell rang, and the Baby-sitters Club silently left the girls' room.

CHAPTER 11

The agency had lit a fire under Kristy. She did call the Kellys and the Jaydells to explain what had happened. They were interested and seemed somewhat friendlier, but Kristy still wasn't sure whether they'd call on the club again. At least the truth had been told.

Then Kristy made plans for us to advertise our club out at Washington Mall. She was already at work on new sandwich boards. Each one would carry a different slogan. We helped Kristy make them up. They were:

YOUNGER IS BETTER!
RESPONSIBILITY + PUNCTUALITY =
THE BABY-SITTERS CLUB
THE FIRST AND FINEST BABY-SITTING
SERVICE
QUALITY CARE FOR KIDS

The first trip to the mall was scheduled for the weekend, but I wouldn't be able to go. I'd be suffering torture at the hands of Dr. Barnes.

On Wednesday afternoon, I baby-sat for Jamie. Something was bothering him. He moped around as if he'd lost his best friend. He had greeted me cheerfully enough when I'd arrived, but as soon as Mrs. Newton carried a bundled-up Lucy out the back door, his face fell. He wandered into the rec room, flipped on the TV, and flung himself onto the couch. He didn't even check to see what was on the channel the television was tuned to. Usually, he wouldn't watch anything except *Sesame Street* or *Mister Rogers' Neighborhood*.

I thought I knew what was wrong. "It must be kind of tough having a new baby at your house," I suggested.

Jamie shrugged. "It's okay."

"I bet she cries a lot."

"Not too much. If Mommy rocks her, she stops."

I thought for a moment. "I remember when my friend Allison's baby sister was born. Allison hated her."

Jamie looked surprised. "I don't hate Lucy," he said.

"Everything is A-OK with the baby?"

Jamie nodded.

"You seem kind of sad," I said after a while.

Jamie let out a sigh that indicated he was carrying the weight of the entire world on his shoulders. "Baby-sitters used to be fun," he said.

I frowned. "What do you mean?"

"Baby-sitters used to play games with me and push me on the swings and color monster pictures and read me stories."

I couldn't get away from the Lucy angle. "And now they're too busy taking care of the baby?"

"No. Too busy watching TV. . . . What are *you* going to watch this afternoon?"

"Me? I'm not going to watch TV. I was going to ask you if you wanted to read *Where the Wild Things Are* and draw pictures of Max's monsters."

Jamie perked up.

"Plus, I brought the Kid-Kit with me."

"You *did*?! I didn't see. Where is it?"

"It's in the living room. But wait a second, Jamie. Tell me more about your baby-sitters. Are you saying that all they do is watch TV?"

"And they" (he leaned over and began to whisper) "they have accidents."

"Accidents?" I whispered back.

"Yeah."

111

"What kinds of accidents?"

He got up and led me across the room to a chair. "Like this," he whispered. He poked at something on the cushion.

I looked at it closely. It was a burn mark. In fact, it was a hole. My eyes widened. "One of your sitters did that?" I asked.

Jamie nodded. "With a—a cigarette." He said "cigarette" as if it were a dirty word. Neither of his parents is a smoker.

"Gosh," I said. "Anything else?"

"Sometimes they talk on the phone. They talk longer than Mommy and Daddy do. . . . Stacey?"

"Yeah?"

"What's a boyfriend?"

I gulped. I hadn't been prepared for that question. "Well," I said thoughtfully, "it's, um, it's a friend who's a boy."

"Am I your boyfriend?" asked Jamie.

"Not exactly. Listen, Jamie. Who baby-sits for you now? Do you know their names?"

Jamie scrunched up his face. "Tammy," he said. "And Barbara. And a boy."

I didn't know Tammy and Barbara or any boy sitters. Maybe they were in high school.

"Well, you know what?" I said. "If you don't like your sitters, you should tell your mommy.

Tell her what you told me, that all they do is watch TV and talk on the phone. And show her the chair. Okay? Can you do that?" I wanted to help the Baby-sitters Club, but I also truly hated to see Jamie so sad.

"Yup."

"Good boy. Now—you don't *really* want to watch the news, do you?" I said, looking at the blaring television set.

"Yuck." Jamie jumped up and switched it off.

"What'll it be?" I asked. "*Wild Things* or the Kid-Kit?"

"Kid-Kit!"

"You got it." I retrieved the Kid-Kit and pulled out the things that would interest an almost-four-year-old. Jamie played happily until Mrs. Newton and Lucy returned.

When I got home that afternoon, I heard the phone ringing. Apparently, Mom was out. I dashed into the kitchen and picked up the receiver. "Hello?"

"Hello, Stacey?"

"Yes?"

"Oh, hi, hon. It's Dr. Johanssen. I was about to hang up."

"Sorry," I said. "I just got home."

"Well, listen, I know your Baby-sitters Club

meets in a little while, but I thought I'd try to catch you now. I need a sitter tonight. It's last minute, but it won't be too late, and Charlotte's been asking for you."

"She has?" I said, feeling very pleased.

"Endlessly," said Dr. Johanssen cheerfully. "Can you come over at seven?"

"Sure!" I replied. (Ordinarily, I'm not allowed to sit both the afternoon and the evening of a school day, but I didn't have much homework, so I knew it would be all right.)

"Terrific. We'll see you then," said Dr. Johanssen.

"Bye." We hung up.

I was pleased for two reasons. Not only was I delighted to have a night job at the Johanssens' (I hadn't had one in quite a while), but I was working on a plan regarding the New York trip, and I needed to discuss something with Dr. Johanssen. I also needed her to answer some questions.

My plan was this: I'd let Mom and Dad take me to their "doctor" on Saturday. I knew what that visit would be like: a lot of questions, especially about my diet and insulin and my medical history, and then maybe a few quick tests, followed by plans for the workup in his clinic on Monday and Tuesday. Just preliminary stuff.

I'd been through it all before. Then I would tell my parents I'd been researching diabetes on my own and that I knew of a doctor *I* wanted to see. That was where Dr. Johanssen came in. I needed her to recommend someone *sensible* to me. Someone who would think that we were handling my disease just fine. Someone like Dr. Werner. Furthermore, the someone needed a fancy office and *lots* of diplomas.

After supper that night, I got the Kid-Kit and a flashlight and took the shortcut through our neighbors' backyards to the Johanssens'. Dr. Johanssen met me at the front door.

"Hi, Stacey," she said. "I'm glad you could come." She closed the door behind me and took my coat. Then she glanced over her shoulder at Charlotte, who was doing her homework at the kitchen table. Dr. Johanssen lowered her voice. "Charlotte has been in a funny mood lately," she told me. "Very quiet, and slightly listless. She says she feels fine, so something's going on that she's not talking about. I have a feeling it's school related, and I've arranged a conference with her teacher. I just wanted you to know so that you won't worry if she seems out of sorts tonight."

"Okay," I replied.

"Mr. Johanssen is working late tonight," Charlotte's mother continued, "and I have a PTA meeting. We'll both be back before nine."

"All right. . . . Dr. Johanssen, when you come home, could I talk to you? We're leaving for New York on Saturday, and I have an idea."

"Certainly, hon. There's something I wanted to tell you anyway." Dr. Johanssen headed into the kitchen. "Well, sweetie," she said to Charlotte, "I won't be late. Finish your homework, and then you can have fun with Stacey until Daddy and I get home. . . . Okay?"

Charlotte nodded.

"Bye, honey."

"Bye." Charlotte barely looked up.

I sat down next to her as her mother left the house. "Gosh, homework in second grade. That's pretty important. *I* didn't have homework in second grade."

"It's just two dumb work sheets," said Charlotte.

"Do you need any help with them?"

She shook her head. "They're easy. It's dumb, dumb homework."

"Well, if it's easy, it won't take you long to finish, right?"

"What do you care?"

"Charlotte!" I exclaimed. "Why are you talking to me like that? If you're mad, you better tell me what I did wrong, because I'm not a mind reader."

Charlotte slouched over her work sheets. "I'm not mad."

"Well, you sound mad." I felt as if I were having a fight with Laine Cummings. "I only wanted to know, because when you finish, we can read some of *The Cricket in Times Square*."

"Oh, *sure*," she said sarcastically.

"Charlotte, what is the matter with you? Your mother said you wanted me to sit for you."

"I wanted you to come over. I didn't want you to baby-sit."

"I don't think I understand."

"Stacey, how come you baby-sit for me?"

"Because I like to," I replied. "You're one of my favorite kids."

Charlotte smiled vaguely. Then she asked, "Why do you *really* sit?"

"Because I like kids. And when I moved here, I wanted to meet people."

"What about the money?"

Money? What had made Charlotte think about *that*? "Well, of course the money's nice. I like to earn money."

"I thought so."

"But I like you, too. I wouldn't baby-sit for just anybody. And I'll tell you something. If your mom and dad called me and said, 'We need you to sit for Charlotte tonight, but we're broke and we can't pay you,' I'd come anyway."

"You would?"

"Yes. I *told* you I like you."

"Some baby-sitters only sit because they want money. They don't care about the kids."

"*Which* baby-sitters?" I asked.

"Mmnns," mumbled Charlotte.

"What?"

"My new ones," she said quietly.

"Who are your new ones?"

"Michelle Patterson, Leslie somebody, and Cathy Morris."

"They all told you that?"

"No. Ellie Morris told me."

"Who's Ellie Morris?"

"Cathy's sister. She's in my class. She hates me."

Aha, I thought.

Charlotte looked at me sadly. "Ellie said, 'Oh, Charlotte, you are the teacher's pet, teacher's pet,' and I said, 'I am not,' and she said, 'Are, too, and you don't have any friends.' And I said, 'I have baby-sitters. They're my friends.' And she said, 'They are not. My sister Cathy doesn't like you.' And I said, 'Then how come she sits for me?' And she said, 'Because your parents pay her a lot of money, stupid.'"

I was beginning to put the pieces together. Charlotte didn't have friends her own age; that much I knew. Apparently, she thought her baby-sitters were her friends, though. Then Ellie had burst her bubble. Yet Charlotte had been asking for me. If I had come over just to visit (not to baby-sit), it would have proved I truly was a friend. No wonder she was upset.

"Hey, Char," I said, "remember when we gave Jamie Newton the Big Brother Party? I invited you. I wasn't baby-sitting for you then."

"Yeah . . ." said Charlotte slowly.

"Also, what do Michelle and Leslie and Cathy do when they baby-sit for you?"

"Watch TV. Talk on the phone. Once Leslie brought her boyfriend over." I raised my eyebrows. "Cathy always does her homework, but she won't help me with mine. She says, 'I'm busy now.'"

"What do *I* do when I baby-sit?"

"Well, you bring the Kid-Kit. We read stories and take walks and play games."

"That's being a friend, isn't it?" I asked.

Suddenly, Charlotte gave me a fierce hug.

"*Yes,*" she said, "I'm sorry I was mad."

"That's all right." I made a mental note to help Charlotte make some friends—some *seven*-year-old friends—in the neighborhood. One of the Pikes was seven, I thought. Then I told her what I had told Jamie that afternoon—that if she didn't like her new sitters, she should talk to her parents. In particular, she should mention that Leslie had invited her boyfriend over.

By the time Dr. Johanssen returned, Charlotte seemed like her old self.

And Charlotte's mother was very helpful. "It's funny," she said when I asked about a doctor. "You know what I was going to tell you? I was going to tell you about this very sensible doctor in New York. I guess we were thinking along the same lines."

I asked about the doctor's office and whether he had a lot of diplomas. He seemed to fit the bill. "Do you think I could get an appointment with him on Saturday afternoon?" I asked. "That's just three days away."

"I'll pull a few strings," said Dr. Johanssen. "And I better explain things to your parents."

"Oh, no. Please don't!" I cried. "It has to be a surprise. Otherwise it'll never work."

"Well, how about if I write a note to your parents? You can give it to them over the week-end—before you see the doctor."

"All right," I said at last. That wasn't quite what I had planned on, but I was willing to compromise. I didn't want Dr. Johanssen to get in any trouble. "That's great," I said, and thanked her.

I ran home feeling excited.

My plan was underway.

CHAPTER 12

Thursday, December 11

Surprise! Today, Stacey called
an emergency club meeting for
lunchtime. That was unexpected for
two reasons. First of all, Kristy
had said no more club business
in school. Second, Kristy calls
emergency meetings at the drop of
a hat, but no other member has
ever called one. Stacey called one,
though, and it was a good thing she
did, because what she told us got
the club ready for the final battle
in the war against the Baby-sitters
Agency.

□ □ □

I read what Mary Anne wrote in our notebook about battles and wars, and I think she was being overly dramatic. However, she was right—it was good that we held that meeting. It started us thinking about some important things.

Finding a place to hold the meeting turned out to be a problem. Kristy acted as if the school were bugged or something.

"How about at a separate table in the cafeteria?" Claudia suggested.

"Are you kidding? Never!" said Kristy. "Someone's *sure* to overhear us."

"Is there an empty classroom we could sit in?" asked Mary Anne.

Kristy rejected the idea. "It's too easy for someone to stand outside the door and eavesdrop."

"I guess the girls' room would—"

"No way. You just hide in one of the stalls and stand on the toilet. No one knows you're there. You could hear everything."

"Well, what about the playground?" I said. "We'll go off by ourselves, but we'll stand out in the open. That way no one can sneak up on us, and we can move away if anyone comes too close."

That was what we decided to do. We ate lunch

quickly and gathered on the playground. Since no one was using the baseball diamond, we stood in the middle of it. It had snowed the night before and there were about three inches covering the ground. My feet were blocks of ice before we even started talking. (In New York City, three inches of snow wouldn't bother to stick. The flakes would melt as soon as they touched the pavement.)

"Okay, Stacey," said Kristy. "So why did you call this meeting?"

"Because we've got a problem."

"Another one?"

"A big one. But it might end up working out well for us," I said.

"That would be a switch," Claudia commented.

"What happened," I began, tucking my mittened hands under my arms in an effort to thaw out my fingers, which were as cold as my toes, "was that I baby-sat twice yesterday. Remember, I told you at the meeting that I had sat for Jamie and he was upset about his new sitters?"

The girls nodded.

"Well, I forgot to tell you that I told Jamie to tell his mother if he doesn't like the sitters. I mean, we can't say anything to the parents, but the kids we sit for can."

"Oh, good idea," remarked Kristy.

"And in the evening I sat for Charlotte, and she was upset, too. So I told *her* to talk to *her* parents. I think that from now on, we should watch for signs that the kids we take care of aren't happy with the Baby-sitters Agency. Then we should encourage them to speak up. They have the right."

The other club members agreed with that wholeheartedly.

We also agreed that agency sitters were inferior to club sitters. We were quality, and they were . . . well, they were not. But we weren't prepared for what we saw on our way home from school that afternoon.

The weather was awful. The sky was gray, and the air was still cold and windy. It was a raw day. The unplowed streets had turned to beds of icy slush. We were all freezing cold and my teeth were chattering. As we rounded the corner to the street that Kristy, Claudia, and Mary Anne live on, we almost bumped into Jamie Newton. He was standing by himself on the narrow strip of grass that runs between the sidewalk and the street.

"Hi-hi!" Jamie called.

"Jamie!" Kristy exclaimed. "What are you doing here?"

"Playing," he replied.

"Well, you're much too near the street. Aren't you supposed to be in your backyard?"

She looked at the rest of us as if to say, what is *wrong* with Mrs. Newton?

"And where are your mittens, Jamie?" I added. "And your hat? It's freezing out here. Is your mother very busy with Lucy today?"

Jamie shook his head. "She's at a meeting. Lucy is asleep."

A car came whizzing down the street then. It sprayed us with slush. I shivered, trying not to think about what might have happened if Jamie had been playing *in* the street.

"Jamie," Mary Anne said suddenly, "do you have a baby-sitter today?"

"Yup."

"What's her name?"

"Barb—no, Cathy."

"Cathy Morris?" I asked.

"Yup."

"Does she know you're out here?" Kristy asked.

Jamie shrugged. "She said I could play outside."

I turned to the club members. "What do you think we should do?" I asked them.

"I'm not sure," Kristy answered slowly.

"Look," I said, kneeling down to Jamie's level. "Can you do two special things? Just for us?"

"Yes," he replied solemnly.

"Good boy. The first thing is to go inside and find your hat and mittens. If you can't reach them, ask Cathy for help. But don't go outdoors without them, okay?"

"Yes."

"The second thing is to play out back if you want to be outdoors. It's dangerous here by the street. Play on your swing, okay?"

"Yes."

We watched Jamie run across his lawn and through his front door before we went on our way.

"Wow," said Kristy. "This is serious. That baby-sitter, whoever the so-called agency found for the Newtons, lets *three*-year-olds play outside on their own. Do you know what could have happened to Jamie?"

"He could have been hit by a car," said Claudia.

"He could have wandered off," said Mary Anne. "You know, the brook's not frozen over yet. What if he fell in?"

"There are worse things," I added. "What

about all the missing kids these days? Someone could have driven by and just scooped him into a car. On a day like this" (I waved my hand around to indicate the disgusting weather) "there probably wouldn't be anyone around to see it happen. The person wouldn't even have to bother trying to *lure* Jamie into the car. He could just—kidnap him."

"That's *awful*," exclaimed Kristy.

"I know."

"Well, I think now we have to do something about the agency. Something more than just telling kids to talk to their parents. The question," Kristy said gravely, "is what? Maybe we should talk to our own parents. My mom usually knows what to do."

"I don't see what the problem is," said Claudia. "If I knew where Mrs. Newton was I'd call her right now and tell her about Jamie. Then I'd call everyone else I could think of."

We had reached Kristy's house and were standing in front of it, shivering and talking.

"No," I said. "I know what Kristy means. If we start calling parents who use the agency, they'll just think we're poor sports, and that we're trying to make the agency look bad because they're taking our business away."

"Oh," said Claudia. "Right."

"Well, let's just go home," Mary Anne suggested. "Maybe we *should* talk to our parents. The important thing is that Jamie's safe for now."

"All right," Kristy agreed uncertainly.

Claudia, Kristy, and Mary Anne went into their houses, and I walked the rest of the way home. I found my mother in the kitchen, reading the paper and having a cup of coffee. "Hi, sweetie," she greeted me. "How was school?"

"Fine. . . . Mom?"

"Yes?"

I had hung up my coat and was pouring myself a glass of milk. I sat down next to her at the table. "If you knew that someone was doing something that could put someone else in danger, what would you do about it?"

Mom looked at me thoughtfully. "I think I need a little more information," she said.

"Well, what if the someone who would be in danger was a little kid, and the someone putting him in danger was someone his parents trusted, but if you told, you would look bad?"

"Stacey Elizabeth," my mother said sharply. "You're not talking about child abuse, are you?"

"Oh, *no*. Nothing like that."

I could see the relief in Mom's eyes. "And," she

asked, "are you talking about any of the girls in your baby-sitting club?"

"No. I swear. I mean, the person *caus*ing the trouble isn't in the club."

"All right. Well, what do you mean about making someone look bad?"

"Making someone look like a poor sport or a tattletale. What's that expression Dad uses?"

"Sour grapes?"

"Yeah. That's it."

"This is just my opinion," said Mom, "because you haven't given me the facts. But offhand, I'd say the person who's going to tell something should risk 'looking bad' if a child really is in danger. There doesn't seem to me to be any question about it. Even if it's a difficult thing to do."

I nodded. "Okay. Thanks, Mom."

I ran upstairs to my parents' bedroom and phoned Kristy.

"I called my mother at work," she told me, "and she said the same thing your mom did, only I told her the whole story. Mary Anne hasn't gotten hold of her father, but Claudia talked to Mimi and *she* said the same thing, too." (Claudia discusses all her problems with Mimi. She and Mimi are very close.)

"Well?" I asked.

"Well . . ." Kristy gulped. "I just saw Mrs. Newton's car drive by. She's home. I guess it's now or never."

Fifteen minutes later, we met on the Newtons' front steps. Nobody wanted to ring the doorbell. After a lot of shuffling around, Claudia finally did it.

Jamie answered the door. "Hi-hi, again," he said. "Mommy's home now!" He sounded absolutely delighted.

"Good," said Claudia. "Your mommy is just the person we want to see."

Mrs. Newton ushered us into the living room. "You look very serious," she said. "Is anything wrong?"

"Actually, yes," said Kristy. She glanced at Jamie, who was trying to climb into his mother's lap. "Could we talk to you alone?"

"Well . . . certainly." Mrs. Newton looked surprised. I couldn't blame her. "Jamie," she said, "go see if *Sesame Street* is on, honey. Okay?"

Jamie left the room.

"We don't exactly know how to tell you this," Kristy began awkwardly, "but I guess we should begin with what happened this afternoon." She glanced at us.

131

Mrs. Newton nodded patiently.

"Well, um, we were walking home from school, and when we got to your house we found Jamie playing outdoors."

"By himself," Mary Anne added.

"Near the street," Claudia added.

"With no hat or mittens," I added.

"He told us Cathy Morris was baby-sitting for him," Kristy continued. "But she was indoors. We don't think she knew where Jamie was. . . . We felt you really ought to know."

Mrs. Newton didn't say a word. She looked horrified.

"We're sorry to be such tattletales," I said nervously, "but we—"

"No, no. Oh, girls, I appreciate your telling me. I'm sure it was hard to do. I'm just—I can't believe—I mean, that was so irre*spon*sible."

I decided to go ahead and tell all. "I knew yesterday that Jamie hasn't liked his new baby-sitters, but we didn't want you to think we were badmouthing our competition. Jamie told me that most of his new sitters just talk on the phone or watch TV. He thought *I* wasn't going to pay any attention to him, either. And one of the sitters smokes, and burned a hole in the chair downstairs. Charlotte Johanssen has been upset, too.

We had a long talk about it last night. She says one of her sitters invites her boyfriend over."

"Well," said Mrs. Newton briskly, "I certainly won't use the agency anymore, although we did find one seventeen-year-old sitter we like very much. I'll continue to call him on his own, but not the others. I have to admit that Jamie hasn't seemed very happy lately, but I blamed it on sibling rivalry—the new baby. Anyway, I'll phone Peggy Johanssen and a few other parents. They'll want to know what you told me. And then I'll call Michelle and Liz, both of them. And Cathy Morris, of course. I wish I knew which one was the smoker."

"Mrs. Newton," Kristy said suddenly, "I know you'll want to call Cathy about this afternoon yourself, but could you let us talk to Liz and Michelle? We have a score to settle with them."

CHAPTER 13

We settled the score first thing the next morning. We marched off to school and planted ourselves outside Liz and Michelle's homeroom.

The girls arrived early.

"Well," said Liz. "Like, look who it is. The Baby Club."

"Like, ha-ha," Kristy replied.

I giggled. Michelle scowled.

"Have you finally come crawling?" Liz asked. "When your club fails, you can always work for us, you know."

"No way," said Kristy. "We're here to talk to you about an important business matter."

"Yeah," I said.

"And what is so important?"

"What is so important," said Kristy, "is that yesterday Cathy Morris was baby-sitting for a three-year-old boy and she let him go outdoors by himself."

"So?"

"So?! We found him playing near the street—with no hat or mittens. We had to send him inside. If we hadn't come along, he might have been hit by a car. Three-year-olds cannot play outside by themselves. And good baby-sitters ought to know that."

"So we won't give Cathy any more jobs," Michelle spoke up. "She doesn't really like baby-sitting anyway."

"That's no surprise," said Claudia.

"What do you mean by that?" snapped Liz.

"I mean," said Claudia, "that the kids *we* know don't like the sitters *you* find."

"Are you saying we're not good baby-sitters?" asked Michelle.

"Well," I said, "a good baby-sitter spends time with the children she sits for. She doesn't ignore them and talk on the phone or just watch TV all the time."

"Oh, we *al*ways play with the kids we take care of. We tell the other sitters to do that, too. Right, Michelle?"

"Oh, *right.*"

"Then," said Kristy, "you must know the kids pretty well by now. A good baby-sitter knows a lot about the children she takes care of. Do you know what Jamie Newton's favorite kind of sandwich is?"

Liz paused. "I only baby-sat for him once," she said.

"It's peanut butter and honey, toasted," said Mary Anne, finding her voice.

"What's Charlotte Johanssen's favorite game?" asked Kristy.

Liz and Michelle glanced at each other. "Candyland?" Michelle said.

"Charlotte's really smart. Her favorite game is Scrabble."

"Have you ever sat for the Marshalls?" asked Claudia.

"*I* have," said Liz. "Two girls: Nina, three, and Eleanor, one." (I really thought she was going to add "So there.")

"Right," said Claudia. "And do you know what it means when Eleanor rubs her ears?"

"That she has an earache?"

"No, it means she's getting hungry."

"Do you remember what Nina is allergic to?" asked Mary Anne.

"For heaven's sake, what is this—Twenty Questions?"

"Come on," said Kristy. "You sat for her. I'll give you a hint. It's a food. What could you have fed her that would have made her break out in hives?"

"I don't know, okay?" Liz said angrily, at the same time that Mary Anne said, "Strawberries."

"What are you trying to prove?" asked Michelle. But she answered her own question. "That you're better baby-sitters than we are?"

"You said it, I didn't," replied Kristy.

"Okay, so you proved it," said Liz. "Now go away and leave us alone."

We did. We gathered in the girls' room. "What do you think that meant?" I asked.

The other club members shook their heads. It had felt like some sort of victory, but we weren't sure. We wondered what had happened when Mrs. Newton called Cathy. We wondered what was going to happen when the parents heard the news about the agency and began talking to their children. We figured we'd hear something over the weekend.

Unfortunately, I was spending that important weekend in New York. My parents picked me up after school on Friday. I was all set. I had packed my bag the night before, and it was in the backseat along with a pillow, a Judy Blume book, an apple, and homework assignments for the following week. More important, I had seen Dr. Johanssen the night before and a special doctor's appointment had been arranged for late Saturday afternoon. Before I left, she had handed me an official-looking envelope with my parents' names typed on the front.

I waved to Claudia, Mary Anne, and Kristy from the car window. "See you on Wednesday!" I called.

My father pulled away from the curb and we began the two-hour drive to New York City. When we reached the highway, I said, "So who are we staying with this time—Aunt Beverly and Uncle Lou or Aunt Carla and Uncle Eric?" I hoped it was Aunt Beverly and Uncle Lou. I liked my cousins Jonathan and Kirsten a lot better than my cousin Cheryl.

Mom and Dad looked at each other and smiled. Then Mom turned around and faced me. "We were going to surprise you when we got to the city, but we might as well tell you now. We're not staying with the Spencers *or* the McGills."

"Yippeee! You mean we're staying in a hotel?" I adore hotels.

"No . . . We're staying with the Cummingses. You can see Laine again."

"With the *Cum*mingses!" I exclaimed. "Do

138

they know what's wrong with me, then? Did you tell them?"

"Yes, we finally told them. It's funny—now that you're so much better, there doesn't seem to be any reason for them *not* to know."

"Does Laine know?"

"Yes. Her parents have told her."

"But, Mom, how could you do that to me? You know Laine hates me. And I hate her."

"Oh, Stacey," said Mom, "that was months ago. I'm sure you and Laine are over that fight, especially now that Laine knows the truth about you."

I slumped down in my seat. "No, we're not," I replied.

"Well, I'm sure you'll feel differently when you see her."

"No, I won't."

Laine didn't, either. When Mrs. Cummings opened the door to their apartment and let Mom and Dad and me in, Laine wasn't in sight. Mrs. Cummings greeted us warmly and showed Mom and Dad into the guest room, where they would be staying. Then she told me to go on into Laine's room. I walked slowly down the hall to her bedroom. Being in the Cummingses' apartment felt strange after such a long time.

Laine's door was closed. A big sign said: KNOCK BEFORE ENTERING.

I knocked.

"Who is it?" Laine called.

"It's Stacey."

No answer.

"Can I come in?"

No answer.

I went in anyway. I threw my duffel bag down on one of the twin beds. Laine was lying on the other bed, reading a book. She didn't look up.

I walked back to the door. "I just want you to know," I said as I started to close the door, "that I'm not any happier to be here than you are to have me. I wanted to stay in a hotel. In fact, staying with Cheryl would have been a picnic compared to this."

Laine finally looked up from her book. "Stacey—"

But I stepped into the hall, slamming the door behind me. I could hear the adults in the living room, so I went into the guest room. It was the only place I could be alone.

Laine and I didn't speak all evening. I noticed, though, that she watched me very carefully, especially at dinner. But there wasn't much for her to see. I cleaned my plate. Dessert was fruit, which

I could eat. I kept my insulin pump out of sight. I'm not sure what Laine was expecting that night, but I didn't faint or throw up, I was neither over-weight nor underweight, and nobody gave me any special attention, food, or favors.

I was as normal as she was, except that I had diabetes.

The next morning, my parents and I left for Dr. Barnes's clinic around eleven o'clock. We wanted to enjoy the city, so we decided to walk. We walked down Central Park West, with the park on our left, and then we turned onto West Sixty-third Street.

The clinic was not far away. It occupied a suite of rooms on the ground floor of a tall, modern apartment building. Mom gave our names to a receptionist in the waiting room and we sat down on a hard couch. We were the only people there.

Fifteen minutes later, a nurse entered the room. She told my parents that Dr. Barnes would be with them shortly. Then she led me down a hall and into an examining cubicle.

And the tests began.

I was examined, poked, and prodded. Blood was drawn. I was fed a specially prepared lunch and more blood was drawn. Then this woman holding a sheaf of papers asked me to do weird things like draw a picture of my family, make up stories about inkblots, and build towers of blocks. I ran on a treadmill and tried to do sit-ups and push-ups. I rode an exercise bicycle. At last, I was given a written test. It might have been an IQ test, but I wasn't sure. Whatever it was, it looked long. My appointment with the other doctor was at five o'clock, and I still hadn't even told my parents about it. At 3:10, I began to feel nervous. At 3:20, I began to perspire. But at 3:30, a nurse came to take the paper away. Whew! Just in time.

I was sent back to the waiting room. I had been at the clinic for four hours and I had not laid eyes on Dr. Barnes.

My parents had, though, and they looked a little confused. I took advantage of that. I spotted a coffee shop across the street from the building the clinic was in. "Let's go get something to drink," I suggested.

When we were seated in a booth, Dad said, "Well, tell us about your day, honey."

I did—briefly.

The waitress brought our order.

As Mom and Dad sipped their coffee, I said carefully, "You know, you guys were right about something."

"What's that?" asked Mom.

"That it's important to learn about diabetes and how to live with it. And so . . . I've been looking into it myself."

"You have?" said Dad. "Good for you."

"Yeah. And I heard about this doctor, Dr. Graham. He's a big authority on childhood diseases, especially diabetes. He's done lots of research and he even started some organization to study diabetes."

Dad raised his eyebrows and nodded his head.

"The thing is," I said, "I have an appointment with him today. It's sort of a . . . surprise. We're supposed to be at his office at five o'clock." I held out the letter from Charlotte's mother. "This is from Dr. Johanssen. I think you better read it now."

"What?" my mother started to say. "Honey, I—"

"Just read it," I said. Dr. Johanssen had shown me the letter before she sealed it in the envelope, so I knew what it said. It explained that we had discussed this new doctor and that I had expressed an interest in seeing him and had asked Dr. Johanssen to help me get an appointment. It said that I had gone to her confidentially, which was why she hadn't contacted my parents personally. She wound up by praising the doctor's work, apologizing to Mom and Dad for any inconvenience, and offering to talk with them when we returned to Stoneybrook.

My parents read the letter together, frowning.

"Stacey, I'm not quite sure what to think of all this," said Dad when the letter had been returned to the envelope.

"I thought you'd be pleased," I said, although that wasn't quite true.

"Well, we are," said Dad. "We're just—we weren't expecting this. We don't know how expensive he's going to be. We don't know anything about him. I wish you'd discussed this with us before you made an appointment."

"You make appointments for me without asking me first," I pointed out.

"True . . ." said Mom. "Dr. Graham. His name sounds familiar. . . . Philip Graham. I think I've heard about him or read about him." She began to look impressed. "He's supposed to be excellent, but very busy and almost impossible to see. You were lucky to get an appointment, Stacey."

"Listen," I said hastily, since Mom seemed so impressed, "his office is way across town at East Seventy-seventh Street and York Avenue. We better get going."

Dad looked at his watch. "We certainly better." He paid the man at the cash register, and we hurried outside and hailed a cab.

I scrambled into the backseat between Mom and Dad. I crossed my fingers. So far, so good.

Dr. Graham's office looked just the way I thought the office of a children's doctor should look. The waiting room was small and cozy, with two big, dumpy couches and lots of child-size chairs. On a little table by a window were some puzzles, a stack of picture books, and several copies of *Cricket* magazine. In a big bin were trucks, cars, dolls, and other toys. I sat down with the latest issue of *Seventeen* and began to read while Mom spoke to the receptionist. In a moment, Dr. Graham himself came out. He was a tall black man with sparkling eyes and a deep voice. I liked him right away.

"Well, Stacey," he said, shaking my hand, "I'm glad to see you. You're my last patient today. These must be your parents."

Mom and Dad and the doctor introduced themselves while Dad tried to apologize for my setting up the appointment without telling them about it.

Dr. Graham said he didn't mind at all. Then he ushered us into his office, which was every bit as fancy and as full of diplomas as I could have hoped. "I'm not going to examine Stacey," he said. "This is a consultation only. I just want to ask some questions."

Some questions! He asked a billion. He asked about my birth, my health before the diabetes was discovered, the course of the disease, and how we were treating it. He asked about the doctors I'd seen and my new doctor in Stoneybrook. He asked me how I was doing in school, how I had adjusted to the move, and whether I was making friends. Finally, he asked my parents to leave the office, and then he asked me some personal questions about how I felt about my doctors, my disease, and even Mom and Dad.

We talked forever, and he wrote down everything I said on a pad of yellow paper. Then he called my parents back into the office.

"Well," Dr. Graham said to them, "you must be very proud of your daughter. I'm sure you feel lucky to have her."

My parents nodded, smiling. "In more ways than one," added Mom.

"I'm glad you realize that," replied Dr. Graham, returning their smile, "because from what you've told me, Stacey was a pretty sick young lady, but she's made excellent progress with her treatment. Quite honestly, without doing any tests, I can see only one problem."

My mother paled slightly.

"What's that?" Dad asked nervously.

"Although Stacey has taken the move to Connecticut and the change of schools and friends in stride, she seems to feel quite unsettled about her disease. She wants to be able to have some control over it, but she's a little afraid of it, is that right, Stacey?"

"Well . . ." I twisted my hands together. It wasn't easy to be with my parents and watch their reactions to what the doctor and I were saying. "I guess. I mean, the thing is, every time I think I understand what's going on, we see some other doctor who tells us to do something different. . . . I asked Dr. Johanssen about Dr. Barnes and his clinic. She said Dr. Barnes might make me go to a psychiatrist, and even change schools." I had to pause and take a deep breath because I felt like I was going to cry. "I don't want to change schools again. I want to stay with Claudia and Kristy and Mary Anne. And I don't want to go to a psychiatrist or start exercise classes or anything else."

There was a few seconds of silence.

Then Dr. Graham spoke quietly. "Dr. Werner is a superb physician," he said. "She has a wonderful reputation and is highly respected. It's my opinion that Stacey couldn't be in better hands—unless they were my own," he added, smiling.

Mom and Dad laughed, but they didn't say anything for a moment. I saw them looking around the office at the diplomas and certificates and awards.

Dad cleared his throat. "I must admit," he said, "that we were a bit perplexed today by some of the things—"

"Many of the things," my mother interrupted.

"—many of the things Dr. Barnes told us. The tests that he's recommending for Monday and Tuesday seem rather . . . unusual. And they're very expensive. Of course, money is no object where Stacey's health is concerned," he added hastily.

"Dr. Graham?" asked Mom. "What do you know about Dr. Barnes's clinic?"

Dr. Graham didn't mince words. "I think it's a lot of bunk. Nothing he'll do will harm Stacey, but I don't think any of it is necessary. It's my opinion that what Stacey needs is some stability. What's most important for her right now is to understand her disease, and she can't do that if each doctor she sees tells her to try something different.

"As I said, I haven't done any tests, but Stacey seems incredibly healthy, considering how ill she was a year ago. And she seems to have a good handle on her insulin levels and her diet."

Mom and Dad looked at each other. They looked at me. "Maybe," said Mom, "it's time Stacey had some more say about her treatments. Do you want to go back to the clinic on Monday?" she asked.

"No," I said, "but I *would* like to see Dr. Werner while we're here. Just for a checkup, if we can get an appointment on Monday."

"You mean you haven't already made one?"

"No," I said, giggling. "And after that we can go *home*, and I can go back to school and my friends and the Baby-sitters Club."

"Well," said Dad, "we'll discuss it tonight."

Everyone stood up then and began shaking hands. I thanked Dr. Graham, and he winked at me and wished me good luck and told me I could call him any time I had questions. He gave me a card with his phone number on it.

And that night we talked, Mom and Dad and I. They didn't leave me out of the discussion. We ate an early dinner in a restaurant and talked for two hours. The decision? No more Dr. Barnes. Mom and Dad hadn't liked him anyway. They said they couldn't promise they'd never take me to some new doctor, but they agreed to hold off for a while, and to let me help make decisions in the future. "Why not?" I said, wolfing down my dinner. "I seem healthy, don't I?"

"As a horse," agreed Dad.

CHAPTER 14

After dinner, we met Mr. and Mrs. Cummings and Laine, and the six of us went to a movie. We reached the theater a little late and couldn't all sit together. Laine and I ended up by ourselves in the back row. We agreed to meet our parents in front of the theater when the movie was over.

While the previews were showing, Laine got up and tiptoed into the lobby. She returned a few minutes later with a soda and a box of M&M's.

"Thanks for asking if *I* wanted something," I whispered huffily.

Laine looked at me in surprise. "You? I thought you couldn't eat any of this stuff."

"I can eat popcorn. I can drink diet soda."

"Well, I didn't know that."

"You would if you ever bothered to speak to me."

"You—"

"Shhh!" The man in front of Laine turned around and glared at us.

Laine lowered her voice. "You don't talk to me, either. You never even told me the truth about your — your sickness."

"Why would I want to talk to someone who ignores me and turns our friends against me and—"

"SHHH!" The man turned around again.

The woman next to him turned around, too. "The movie is starting," she said, "and I'd like to hear what's going on."

I stood up. "Will you please let me by, Laine?" I asked super-politely. "I'd like to get something to eat."

I stalked out of the dark theater — but I wasn't alone. Laine was right behind me. I ignored her and stepped up to the snack counter. "A small Diet Coke and a small popcorn, please," I said to the boy behind the counter.

He told me the price.

I gulped. I'd forgotten how expensive things were in New York.

The boy pushed my order across the counter. "Here you go."

I unfolded my money. I was seventy-five cents short.

I blushed furiously.

"Here's seventy-five cents." Laine dropped three quarters into the boy's outstretched hand.

"Thanks," I mumbled.

"Stacey?" Laine said as I turned around, carrying my food.

"Yeah?"

"I'm sorry."

She didn't have to say what she was sorry about. I knew. "You are?"

"Yeah."

"I'm sorry, too. I guess I should have told you what was wrong, but Mom and Dad weren't telling anyone but family. . . . How come you stopped being my friend?"

Laine looked at her feet. "I don't know." She sat down on a bench outside the entrance to the ladies' room.

I sat down next to her, trying to balance the soda and the container of popcorn.

"I mean, I do know, I think. This is going to sound funny, but I was jealous."

"*Jealous? Of me?* You wanted to be sick?"

"Well, no. Of course not. I think if I had known what was wrong, I would have acted different. But you were getting so much attention. The teachers were always asking how you felt and giving you extensions on our assignments. And you got to miss so much school."

"Laine, I nearly had to stay back."

"You're kidding. I didn't know that. . . . Well, anyway," she went on, "remember Bobby Reeder?"

I nodded.

"He said he thought you were contagious. I don't know why I believed him, but I did. And since I was your best friend, I was *positive* I was going to get it, whatever it was. I was so scared. I just didn't want to be around you anymore. When my mother and father finally found out about our fight, they were sort of mad. We talked about it, but I didn't know how to apologize to you. That's why I never wrote after you moved to Connecticut. Besides, I didn't think you'd accept my apology. If *I* were you, I wouldn't want *me* for a friend."

I giggled. "Well," I said after a moment, "I *was* pretty mad. You did some mean things. But I guess it would have helped if I'd told you the truth. You know, lately I've been remembering New York a lot. And every now and then, I've thought, 'Gosh, I wonder if Laine would know. . . .' A couple of times I almost decided to write you a letter."

"What kinds of things were you wondering about?"

"Well, for instance, remember Deirdre Dunlop, and how we always said she'd be the first one in our class to outgrow her training bra? So, I was wondering—did she?"

Laine laughed, nearly snorting her root beer up her nose. "Yes!" she exclaimed. "And remember Lowell Johnston?"

"Yeah."

"The day Deirdre came in wearing her new bra, he asked her for a date."

"You're kidding!"

"No. Honest. Cross my heart."

I kept asking questions and Laine kept answering them. I realized how much I had missed her.

The next thing we knew, people were pouring out of the theater and into the lobby. We'd missed the whole movie!

"Oh, well," I said to Laine. "It was worth it. We can see this movie anytime, but on Monday, I'll be leaving."

We tossed our empty cups and boxes in a trash can and waited in front of the theater for our parents.

That night, Laine and I talked until 2:30. We were tired the next morning, but we wanted to make the most of our day. We ate breakfast by ourselves at Leo's Coffee Shoppe around the corner from Laine's apartment building. Then we took a walk in Central Park. In the afternoon, the Cummingses and Mom and Dad and I went to *Paris Magic*. It was the best musical I'd ever seen. Afterward, we ate dinner at one of my favorite restaurants, Joe Allen.

When we got back to Laine's apartment, she and I wanted to have another night of secrets and chitchat, but Mrs. Cummings said, "Lights out at ten o'clock," since Laine had to go to school the next day. By the time we went to sleep, I felt as if two huge weights had been lifted from my chest. One weight was the fight with Laine. The other was Dr. Barnes and his clinic. I didn't have to worry about either one anymore.

Mom called Dr. Werner's office early Monday morning. The receptionist said she could squeeze me in between patients, so I saw Dr. Werner at 10:30. She said I was doing fine.

And then we went home. I couldn't believe how happy I was to see Stoneybrook again. And I couldn't wait for school to let out so I could talk to the other members of the Baby-sitters Club. Luckily, I didn't have to wait long.

As soon as I saw kids riding their bikes up my street, I called the Kishis.

Mimi answered the phone.

"Hi, Mimi," I said. "It's Stacey."

"Stacey! You are at home? Claudia said that you would not be back until Wednesday. Everything is all right, I hope."

"Oh, yes! It's fine. Great, in fact! I'm glad to be home. Is Claudia back from school yet?"

"She is just walking in the door. Please wait and I will call her to the phone."

"Hello?" said Claudia, after several seconds.

"Claud, it's me, Stacey! I'm back early! I'm finished with Dr. Barnes. Did anything happen over the weekend? Did you go to the mall? Did any parents call Liz or Michelle?"

"Quite a few," Claudia replied smugly. "Charlotte and Jamie and the other kids told their parents *ev*erything. You should have seen the faces those girls put on in school today! If looks could kill, you'd be the only member of the Babysitters Club left."

"Wow," I said, giggling.

"I think our meeting this afternoon will be pretty interesting."

"Can I come over now? I can't wait any longer."

"Sure!"

I ran right over to Claudia's house. On the way, I passed Sam Thomas. I realized I'd barely thought about him recently. I'd been too wrapped up in doctors and the Baby-sitters Club. Besides, I was looking forward to going to the Snowflake Dance with Pete Black.

"Hi, Stacey!" Sam called.

"Hi, Sam!" I replied, and ran on.

Claudia met me at her front door and we went upstairs to her room. The girls had not, as it turned out, gone to the mall with their sandwich boards. Too much had been happening with the Baby-sitters Agency and the angry parents. They had decided to try to go the next weekend — if it was even necessary.

The phone began ringing at 4:30, an hour before our meetings start. Kristy and Mary Anne hadn't arrived yet. I answered the first call. It was Mrs. Newton. "Hi, Stacey," she said. "I'm holding a meeting of the Literary Circle at my house on Friday afternoon, and I need someone to watch Lucy and keep Jamie busy for a couple of hours."

Watch Lucy! I was thrilled. "Oh, I'll do it!" I said. "What time?"

"Three-thirty to five-thirty."

"Great! I'll be there."

"By the way, Stacey, I thought you'd like to know that I had a talk with Cathy Morris. I hope I wasn't too hard on her. I explained all the responsibilities that are involved in baby-sitting and told her how upset I was about last week. I think she honestly didn't realize what she was doing wrong. She also told me she just found an after-school job at Polly's Fine Candy. She seems excited about it."

"Well, good," I said. "She'll probably earn more money that way."

"I also called the Johanssens, the Marshalls, the Pikes, the Spencers, the Gianmarcos, the Dodsons, and even Kristy's mother, just in *case* she would ever think of using the agency for David Michael. All the parents agreed that, if nothing else, they ought to know their baby-sitters in advance, and not trust the agency to find sitters for them. And I heard a number of complaints from other parents. Jamie and Charlotte weren't the only unhappy children. I want you to know how grateful we are that you girls were brave enough to come forward and tell us what was going on."

"Well," I said, "it wasn't easy, but I'm glad we did it."

A minute later, I got off the phone and began bubbling over with everything Mrs. Newton had said.

But Claudia just glared at me.

"What?" I said. "What's the matter?"

"Stacey, you took that job Mrs. Newton offered. You know the rules."

Oops. "Oh, yeah," I said. "Sorry." The rule is that every job that comes along must be offered to all the members of the club before someone takes it. I had just broken one of our most important rules.

"I'd like to take care of Lucy, too, you know," said Claudia. "And I bet Kristy and Mary Anne would feel the same way."

"I'm sorry," I said again. "I just forgot. I was so excited."

"Oh, it's okay," replied Claudia. "I'd be pretty excited if *I* were you. Besides, I've broken that rule often enough myself."

I grinned. That was true.

During the next half hour, both Mrs. Marshall and Mr. Johanssen called with last-minute jobs they had had agency sitters lined up for, but had canceled over the weekend.

Kristy and Mary Anne arrived. We were offered four more jobs. One was with a new client. At six o'clock we got off the phone.

"I wonder if anybody will call us at home tonight," said Mary Anne.

"Probably," answered Kristy. "With Christmas so close, everybody is going to parties, dinners, concerts. . . . This may be our busiest season."

"Well," I said, "it's been tough, but we hung in there and beat out the agency."

"More important," added Kristy, "we beat them because we're *good* baby-sitters."

"We won the battle *and* the war," said Mary Anne.

"We're the best!" exclaimed Claudia.

"I feel like we need a cheer," I said. "You know, 'Rah, rah, rah! Sis, boom, bah! . . . Something . . . something. . . The Baby-sitters Club! Hooray!'"

"Would you settle for junk food?" asked Claudia. She removed a bag of gumdrops (and a smushed package of Saltines for me) from under the cushion of her armchair. "We ought to congratulate ourselves and celebrate."

The four of us looked at each other. "Congratulations," we said solemnly.

"We made it," I added.

Claudia passed around the food.

CHAPTER 15

Ring, ring.

"Hello?"

"Hello . . . Stacey?"

"Yes . . . Laine, hi! Oh, I'm so glad you called. Hang on just a sec?" I rested the phone on the kitchen table. "Mom, it's Laine. I'm going to talk to her in your room, okay? Could you hang up the phone when you hear me get on?" I raced upstairs and closed the door to my parents' bedroom. "I'm on, Mom." I heard a click as she hung up the phone. "All right, now we can talk," I told Laine. "So what's going on?"

"Well, I wanted to know what happened with your baby-sitting club. Last weekend, you said something was going on with some agency."

"Oh, you won't believe it! The agency went out of business!"

"You are kidding me!"

"No, honest," I said. "The parents stopped

calling the agency because they decided they couldn't trust Liz and Michelle—you know, those two girls—to find good sitters. But guess what? Okay, so Claudia tells me this on Monday. We go to school on Tuesday and there's Liz, standing on the lawn, carrying a sign that says 'Makeovers Inc.,' and next to her is Michelle with a bunch of flyers. She's passing them out, and Kristy, the president of our club, is so curious she goes and takes one even though Michelle is looking at Kristy like she's a snake or a roach or something."

Laine giggled.

"We read the flyer," I continued, "and Liz and Michelle *already have a new business*! You call them and pay them five dollars, and they show you how to put on makeup, figure out the best way to fix your hair, that kind of thing. It's perfect for them, since that's all they care about. Then, for another five dollars, they'll take you shopping and help you pick out new clothes and jewelry and stuff. They even have special rates before school dances and holidays. Those girls are smart, Laine. They'll probably earn more money doing that than lining up sitting jobs for their friends.

"Oh, gosh," I went on. "I have so much to tell you! Yesterday, I got to sit for Lucy Newton, the new baby I told you about."

"Really?" squealed Laine. "You got to *sit* for her?"

"Well, sort of. Her mother was at home, but I did watch her and her brother for two hours while Mrs. Newton held a meeting. And I got to hold her and give her a bottle. It was great! I can't wait until I can really baby-sit for her. Oh, and you know what else?"

"What?"

"Remember Charlotte Johanssen, the little girl who's having trouble with the kids at school?"

"Yeah?"

"Well, her parents had a conference with her teacher and they've decided to skip her into third grade. The work in second grade is too easy for Charlotte, and her classmates don't like her because she always does her assignments so fast and never makes any mistakes. Her teacher thinks she'll do better starting over in a new class where the kids don't know her and the work will be more challenging. Charlotte seems really excited. She's going to switch to the new class after Christmas."

"Well, that's good. I really wish I could meet all these people, Stace. I feel like I know them alr—just a sec. . . . Stacey, my mom says I have to get off in two minutes."

"Oh, no!" I cried. "Well, wait. I'll talk fast. I went to the Snowflake Dance with Pete and we had a great time. I got a new dress. And for Christmas, Mom and Dad are going to give me a phone for my room, just so I can call you! And I want to know exactly how many times Deirdre and Lowell have gone out, counting everything, even trips to the library. And what did you ask for for Christmas?"

"I—Mom says she has to use the phone. I've got to get off."

"But, Laine, you didn't have time to tell me *any*thing about you."

"I know."

"Hey, you'll be the first person I call when I get my phone."

"Okay! Great!" Laine dropped her voice to a whisper. "Mom doesn't know it, but I'm going to call you on Christmas Day, okay?"

"Terrific!"

"Bye, Stacey."

"Bye! Thanks for calling."

"Talk to you soon."

"I can't wait."

"Me, neither."

"Me, neither."

"How are we going to end this?"

"I don't know."

"I miss you."

"I miss you, too."

"Now I *really* have to get off."

"Bye, Laine."

"Bye, Stacey."

We hung up. A huge grin spread across my face. I had a great idea. If Laine ever came to visit me in Stoneybrook, I would make her an honorary member of the Baby-sitters Club.

About the Author

Ann M. Martin's The Baby-sitters Club has sold over 180 million copies and inspired a generation of young readers. Her novels include the Newbery Honor Book *A Corner of the Universe*, *A Dog's Life*, and the Main Street series. She lives in upstate New York.

Keep reading for a sneak peek at the next book
from The Baby-sitters Club!

MARY ANNE SAVES THE DAY

"Yes," Kristy was saying. "Yes. . . . Oh, Jamie *and*
Lucy." (Claudia and Stacey and I squealed with
delight.) "Friday . . . six till eight. . . . Of course. I'll
be there. Great. See you."

Kristy would be there?! Claud and Stacey and
I stared at each other. I don't know what my face
looked like, but I could see a mixture of horror
and anger on the others' faces.

Kristy, however, was so thrilled at the possibility of taking care of Lucy, at first she didn't
even realize what she'd done.

"I'm so excited! Six till eight. . . . I'll probably get to give Lucy a bottle—" Kristy broke off, finally realizing that nobody else looked nearly as happy as she did. "Oh," she said. "Sorry."

"*Kristy!*" exclaimed Claudia. "You're supposed to offer the job around. You know that. It's *your* rule. I'd like to sit for Lucy, too."

"So would I," added Stacey.

"Me, too." I checked our record book. "And we're all free then."

"Boy," said Claudia sullenly. "Some people around here sure are job-hogs."

"I *said* I was sorry," exclaimed Kristy. "Besides, look who's talking."

"What do you mean, look who's talking?" said Claudia.

"Well," Stacey began, and I could tell that she was trying to be polite, "you *have* done that a lot yourself. Remember that job with Charlotte Johanssen? And the one with the Marshalls?"

"And the one with the Pikes?" I added cautiously. It was true. Claudia had forgotten to offer a lot of jobs.

"Hey, what are you guys? Elephants? Don't you ever forget anything?"

"Well, it *has* been a problem," said Kristy.

"I don't believe this!" cried Claudia. "*You*" (she pointed accusingly at Kristy) "break one of our rules, and everyone jumps on *me*! I didn't do anything. I'm innocent."

"*This* time," muttered Stacey.

"Hey," said Claudia. "If you're so desperate to have new friends here in Stoneybrook, don't argue with the ones you've got."

"Is that a threat?" exclaimed Stacey. "Because if it is, I don't need you guys. Don't forget where I'm from."

"We *know*, we *know*—New York. It's all you talk about."

"I was *going* to say," Stacey went on haughtily, "before I was interrupted, that I'm tough. And I'm a fighter, and I don't need anybody. Not stuck-up job-hogs" (she looked at Claudia) "or bossy know-it-alls"—Kristy—"or shy little babies." Me.

"I am not a shy little baby!" I said, but as soon as I said it, my chin began to tremble and my eyes filled with tears.

"Oh, shut up," Kristy said.

But I'd had it. I jumped to my feet. "No, *you* shut up," I shouted at Kristy. "And you, too," I said to Stacey. "I don't care how tough you are or how special you think you are because of your dumb diabetes, you have no right—"

"Don't call Stacey's diabetes dumb!" Claudia cut in.

"And don't bother to stick up for me," Stacey shouted back at Claudia. "Don't do me any favors."

"No problem," Claudia replied icily.

"Hey," said Kristy suddenly. "Who were you calling a bossy know-it-all before?"

"Who do you think?" replied Stacey.

"Me?!" Kristy glanced at me.

"Maybe I am shy," I said loudly, edging toward the door. "And maybe I am quiet, but you guys can*not* step all over me. You want to know what I think? I think you, Stacey, are a conceited snob; and you, Claudia, are a stuck-up job-hog; and you, Kristin Amanda Thomas, are the biggest, bossiest know-it-all in the world, and I don't care if I never see you again!"

I let myself out of Claudia's room, slamming the door behind me so hard that the walls shook. Then I ran down the stairs. Behind me, I could hear Claudia, Stacey, and Kristy yelling at each other. As I reached the Kishis' front hall, Claudia's door slammed again. Two more pairs of legs thundered down the stairs.

I ran home, half hoping that either Kristy or Stacey would call after me. But neither one did.

Want more baby-sitting?

ANN M. MARTIN #1
THE BABY-SITTERS CLUB
Kristy's Great Idea

ANN M. MARTIN #2
THE BABY-SITTERS CLUB
Claudia and the Phantom Phone Calls

ANN M. MARTIN #3
THE BABY-SITTERS CLUB
The Truth about Stacey

ANN M. MARTIN #4
THE BABY-SITTERS CLUB
Mary Anne Saves the Day

ANN M. MARTIN #5
THE BABY-SITTERS CLUB
Dawn and the Impossible Three

ANN M. MARTIN #6
THE BABY-SITTERS CLUB
Kristy's Big Day

THE BABY-SITTERS CLUB